TITUBA
of Salem Village

ANN PETRY

HarperTrophy®
A Division of HarperCollinsPublishers

Also by Ann Petry

HARRIET TUBMAN: *Conductor on the Underground Railroad*

Harper Trophy® is a registered trademark of HarperCollins Publishers Inc.

Tituba of Salem Village
COPYRIGHT © 1964 by Ann Petry

LC Number 64-20691
ISBN 0-06-440403-X (pbk.)
First Harper Trophy edition, 1991.

TO MY UNCLE

Frank B. Chisholm

"I cannot but condemn this method of the Justices, of making this touch of the hand a rule to discover witchcraft; because I am fully persuaded that it is sorcery, and a superstitious method, and that which we have no rule for, either from reason or religion. The Salem Justices, at least some of them, do assert, that the cure of the afflicted persons is a natural effect of this touch."

LETTER OF THOMAS BRATTLE
Boston, October 8, 1692

Chapter 1

T HERE WAS nothing to indicate to the slave Tituba that this morning in November would be unlike other mornings she had known in Bridgetown. The sun was out. The island of Barbados lay like a jewel sparkling in the sea. Its yellow-white coral-encrusted coast line blazed in the brilliant light. Tituba could see part of the shore line from the windows of Susanna Endicott's kitchen because the house sat on the edge of Carlisle Bay, just where it made a wide inward curve.

The slave John, Tituba's husband, had been fishing and he was showing her the red snappers he had caught. He had carried them into the kitchen in a big hand-woven basket. The basket was a deep dark brown, almost as dark as his hands, and the fish as he took them out of the basket were silvery by contrast. He had covered the fish with leaves to keep them cool.

"Good eating," John said, holding one of the big fish up for Tituba's inspection. He was a tall, powerfully built man with broad shoulders. He wore only a pair of white cotton trousers rolled up to the knee. He was barefooted. He leaned over the basket and then straightened up with a fluid, easy movement that made the muscles on his back ripple under the dark brown skin. He smiled, and his face which had looked dark and severe in repose was lightened and brightened by the smile.

Tituba took one of the big fish in her hands and laughed. "It feels like I was holding a long wiggle," she said and dropped the fish in the basket. She was short compared to John, but she held herself so erect that she looked taller than she really was. Her magnificent posture was due to the fact that she liked to carry baskets balanced on her head like the market women. Her hair was completely covered by a neatly wound white turban. She was wearing a pale blue cotton dress. The sleeves were rolled above her elbows revealing sturdy arms, the skin a smooth dark brown. She was barefooted, too.

They were so absorbed in their admiration of the fish that they both turned, startled, when Mistress Susanna Endicott came into the kitchen.

Tituba said, "You wanted something, mistress?" She had never known the mistress to be up so early in the morning. She glanced at her quickly and then away. The mistress's dark hair was disordered. She was still wearing her night clothes. She had the rumpled look of someone who has slept badly. Her eyelids were reddened and slightly swollen, suggesting that she had been crying.

"I—uh—I," she said and stopped. She patted her hair and then smoothed it with her hands. "I—uh—I should have told you yesterday—but—uh—I couldn't—" She paused, sighed, making a tremulous sound, a shivering kind of sound in the absolute stillness in the kitchen. "I needed money. I had to have money. And so—uh—I have sold you. Both of you."

Tituba made a sound of protest, "Ah——" The beat of her heart kept increasing. She could feel it thumping, thumping inside her chest. Her mind filled with questions. To whom had the mistress sold them? She was a wealthy widow. Why had she so suddenly needed money? Tituba wondered why she had had no feeling of foreboding to indicate that something dreadful was going to happen.

John said, frowning, "Who bought us, mistress?"

"I couldn't help it," the mistress said. "I couldn't help it. I needed money right away."

"Who bought us, mistress?" he repeated.

" 'Tis a minister. The Reverend Samuel Parris. He's been in trade here in Barbados. And he didn't do well. So he's leaving. He's going to be a minister in Boston in the Bay Colony."

"When did you sell us, mistress?" Tituba asked.

"Yesterday."

"Yesterday?" Tituba echoed the word, trying to think, to remember what yesterday was like. It was just another sunny, warm day. She had gone swimming in the inlet beyond the house. The water was so clear you could see the tiniest pebble way down at the bottom.

The mistress had been her usual self—nervous, excitable, restless. Tituba had belonged to Mistress Endicott ever since she was fourteen. She and John were quite accustomed to her ways. Tituba was nineteen when the mistress became a widow, rich enough to live as she pleased and own as many slaves as she pleased. When John's master died, the mistress bought John at Tituba's urging. Shortly afterwards she and John were married.

During the ten years of their married life, they had

been very happy with the mistress. They were used to her. She was always giving parties or going to parties. She liked to stay up late at night and stay in bed until late in the day. She liked to play card games. She liked to have her fortune told. She'd had a gypsy woman teach Tituba how to tell fortunes with cards.

Tituba said hesitantly, "When are we to leave Barbados, mistress?"

Mistress Endicott averted her head, fumbled for, and found a small white handkerchief which she pressed against her nose. She crossed the kitchen, looked out at the bay. "This morning," she said in a muffled voice, "in a little while. Reverend Parris is leaving on the *Blessing*. It's in the bay. You can see its sails from the window."

Tituba thought, If I had known I would have run off into the hills with John. Later we could have gotten a boat and gone to another island and lived free in the hills and woods of some other island. She says our new master is going to be a minister in Boston in the Bay Colony. Where is Boston in the Bay Colony? She reached for John's hand and held it tight. At least they would be together in this strange land where they were going.

"Come," the mistress said. "I have something for both of you. Brought from England. Never worn. We have to hurry. Reverend Parris will be here soon."

They followed her into her bedroom. At the foot of the great bedstead there was a huge carved chest. The mistress opened it, then knelt down and took out a dark brown shawl, very soft, very thick, and handed it to Tituba. Then she reached farther into the chest and drew out a dark brown wool dress and a heavy cloak of deep dark green. "Wear the dress," she said, "and carry the cloak and the shawl over your arm."

She handed John a woolen cap, a greatcoat, and a pair of dark woolen pants and a jacket of the same dark, heavy woolen cloth. "Put these pants on. It will be cold." She reached farther down in the chest. "Here are good stout shoes for both of you. You must wear them. There will be snow in Boston. You can not go barefoot in the snow."

She fell to sobbing, still on her knees, her head resting on the edge of the great carved chest. "You were my jewels," she said, "my friends—my dearest friends."

"It is indeed a sorrowful thing," Tituba said, shaking her head. We were her jewels? she thought. She still wears diamonds on her soft white hands and golden bracelets on her wrists, her slender neck is encircled by a turquoise necklace. We were her friends?

Tituba put on the heavy woolen dress, and felt her skin prickle, and sweat break out on her body. She wound a clean, white linen turban around her head and then went to pack their belongings in a bundle. John came into the kitchen, wearing the dark wool pants. He was fingering the fabric as though he were trying to keep it away from his skin. He was carrying the jacket and the greatcoat.

He was ready sooner than she had expected. She had planned to spend a few quiet moments sitting in the kitchen. She wanted to impress it on her memory—the big fireplace, the black iron cooking pots, the high ceiling, and the view of the bay like a part of the kitchen, and a glimpse of the little inlet where she went swimming early in the morning. She could ease her feet, too, as she sat— her feet pained in the shoes. She tucked the thunderstone into the front of her dress. It was wrapped in layers and layers of cloth just as it was when it was given to her by a very old man way up in the hills. She had begun to tie up the bundle she was going to carry when the mistress came into the kitchen with the Reverend Samuel Parris.

They said good-bye to the mistress quickly, and then she and John walked out of the house with the new master. Tituba felt herself short beside him, and because his skin was so white and unhealthy looking—no tinge of pink to suggest blood flowed in his veins—she felt her own skin to be very dark.

He was tall and thin and dressed in black clothes. He spoke abruptly, his manner as hurried as his speech. He headed towards the dock, walking fast. He said his wife was sickly and that she had already boarded the ship, the brig *Blessing*, and that they would get aboard now immediately because the ship was to sail within two hours if not before. All signs were propitious; the weather was clear; there was little or no wind.

Before they got on the ship, they would pray for a safe passage. To her astonishment, he knelt right down on the dock and gestured to them to kneel, too. He began to pray in a loud harsh voice. People turned and stared at him, and stared at her and at John. She thought how foolish they must look, down on their knees, in the middle of all the hustle and bustle caused by the loading and unloading of ships, the comings and goings of sailors and slaves and traders. It was hot in the sun. Her feet hurt in the heavy shoes. She had the woolen shawl and the heavy cloak over one arm, and that arm was drenched with sweat—she could feel sweat pouring down her body. She looked at John, and his face and forehead were wet with sweat.

Finally the master said, "Amen," and stood up.

A sailor standing nearby said, "Amen," in a loud voice, and when the master turned to look at him, he added, "Thank God, Parson, it's finally and at last 'Amen.' Your prayer was overlong. We've a use for that bit of dock you were using as a prayer rug."

The master glared at the sailor and said sternly, "You are an impious young man." Then he turned to Tituba and said, "You weren't paying attention."

"No, master," she said calmly. "This is not our religion."

He said, "You're not Christians?"

"Yes, master. We are Christians, but we have our own religion—we belong to the Church of England."

"This will never do, never do," he said. "Heathens—heathens—come along."

Once they were aboard the *Blessing* he hurried them to the captain's cabin, where he borrowed a Bible, got a bowl of water, and said a prayer over the water.

"What's your last name?" he asked.

"We have no last name, master," John said.

"You have to have a last name. You're from Barbados, and it's part of the West Indies—so—well—your last name will be Indian. John Indian and Tituba Indian."

In spite of John's protests, he baptized them and wrote their names down in the back of the ship's Bible and the date, November 10, 1688. Then he wanted to know if they were married.

John said, "Yes, master. We were married in Mistress

Susanna Endicott's church in Bridgetown. Ten years ago. She belongs to the Church of England and so do we—at least we did."

The master said he was certain it wasn't a proper marriage service. He beckoned to them to come outside with him. He married them again while they stood on the deck in the hot sun.

When he finished, Tituba backed away from him because the shadow of this tall thin man fell slantways over her body, and she thought it boded ill for her and John to start out this way with the master's shadow over them, blotting out the sun.

It always seemed to her afterwards that one moment she had seen the dock in Bridgetown—all brilliant sunlight, blue water, blue sky, and warm air—and the town lying behind it—the town filled with life, houses and shops and warehouses—and then everything vanished, and there was nothing to be seen but water. The sky was gray, and the water was a darker, more ominous gray, and the air kept getting colder and colder.

The island didn't vanish suddenly. It was simply that she went to look after her new mistress, who was sick, and by the time she finished making her as comfortable as she could, they were far out to sea, and there was nothing to be seen but the ocean, no land, no other ship.

She nursed this new mistress as best she could. She gave her water, made a thin gruel which she fed her from a spoon whenever she could persuade her to sip some of it. She wiped her face and her hands, and wondered what was wrong with her—she was so thin and so white and sad-looking, and she coughed so much.

Betsey Parris, the master's five-year-old daughter, and Abigail Williams, his eight-year-old niece, Tituba, John, and the master were all assigned to the same small cabin. It was cold and damp in the cabin. The air was foul. Tituba decided she had never been so miserable in her entire life. Sometimes they ran into storms, and she thought the brig would split in two from the force of the waves and the sails would split along with the brig.

Whenever the boat rocked violently, the master got down on his knees, motioned to Tituba and the children to follow his example, and then lifted his voice loudly in prayer. He had told Tituba that she must keep her eyes closed when he prayed, that she was to pray with him—silently, of course—her mind and her thoughts lifted in silent supplication to the Lord. Quite often Tituba opened her eyes wide enough to be able to see the outline of the thin body of the sick woman, lying in the bunk under a blanket; the two children with hands raised, palms together, pointing upward toward heaven; and the master with his eyes tightly closed as he lifted his harsh voice in prayer. She noticed that though Betsey kept her eyes tightly shut, Abigail didn't—sometimes she smiled, and once she took to coughing so that the master frowned and ended his prayer abruptly.

Even when the sun was out, the water was rough and the air was bitterly cold. Each day it got colder. Finally she wrapped Mistress Endicott's thick, soft shawl tight around her head and shoulders, held it close to her shivering body. It was just as though she were sitting in the sun in the courtyard of the house in Bridgetown, warm in the sun, no chill wind, no draughts. The smaller of the two girls, Betsey Parris, seemed to feel the cold much worse than her cousin Abigail. Tituba often sat in the cabin with little Betsey on her lap, the soft shawl warming both of them. Betsey would burrow under the shawl, letting it cover her face, until only the yellow hair was visible. She was a fragile child, delicately boned, very thin. She had pale blue eyes, the soft, slow-moving eyes of a dreamer.

Abigail Williams was taller, sturdier. Her eyes were bright blue; the expression was alert, lively. Whenever she saw Betsey snuggled under Tituba's shawl, she frowned and tried to find an unfinished task for Betsey.

Tituba quickly became aware that there was a difference in the way the master treated the children. At first, she thought it was because Abigail was the oldest and the strongest, and therefore was naturally expected to do more than the younger child. But the master made it quite clear that the difference in treatment stemmed from the fact that bright-eyed Abigail was his wife's orphaned niece whereas Betsey was his daughter, his only child.

He always referred to Betsey as "my little daughter" and to Abigail as "my wife's orphan niece." He reminded Abigail of her position in the family by saying, "You must work hard at your tasks so that you do not become a burden to us, Abigail." Sometimes he said, "You must practice being grateful, Abigail. Remember you are an orphan."

John helped the sailors keep the ship clean, helped the man who did the cooking. Tituba thought this an utter waste of time, to have a man who prepared the food. The result did not suggest that anyone had prepared it. Day after day they ate the same lumpy corn porridge, the same tough pieces of salt beef. This diet was varied by the addition of partly freshened salt codfish.

John brought bits of news. He said they were the only passengers. "They say our new master came to the island to trade. He lost almost everything he had because two ships carrying some of his goods went down at sea. They say he's writing sermons. That's why he writes so much."

Tituba nodded, glad of an explanation. The master carried his papers in a small wooden chest—he called it a writing chest. He set it up in front of him and rested his paper on it. Sometimes he frowned when he wrote; sometimes he bit his lower lip. When he sat in that small enclosed space with them, writing, he seemed to fill the cabin. The children talked to the mistress, and she replied, almost whispering. She was quite weak and she didn't have the strength to speak with vigor. Whenever she spoke, the master would turn away from his writing and look at her, as though he were disturbed by the sound.

John said, "The master wants to get a church in Boston. He thinks the captain may be able to help him."

Tituba said, "That's why he made a show of us on the dock while he prayed, and made a show of us in the captain's cabin while he changed us from one kind of Christians to another kind of Christians, and made a show of us on the deck of the brig while he married us again. He was showing everybody—captain and crew—that he was a minister."

"I tried to tell him—"

"He doesn't listen to what people say. He just goes right on doing what he wants to do." She shook her head. "We should have run away."

"When? On the dock there in Bridgetown? How far do you think we would have gone before we were stopped?" He was silent for a moment, and then he said quietly but insistently, "Remember, always remember, the slave must survive. No matter what happens to the master, the slave must survive."

"Survive?" she said. "What does that mean?" John had belonged to a merchant in Bridgetown, an old man who had bought him when he was a small boy. He had educated John, teaching him to read and to write and to work with numbers, because he said he could not have ignorant people in his household. Thus John often used words that she did not understand.

"It means that the slave must stay alive and in good health, no matter what happens to the master." He hesitated, as though making up his mind, and then he said, "The sailors say there are Indians, wild Indians, in the Colony. Sometimes they kill the white man. Sometimes the crops fail and there isn't enough to eat. In spite of these things, you and I must stay alive and in good health."

Tituba went back to the cabin, thinking how easy it was to say "the slave must survive." How could slaves survive the cold of this long ocean trip? How could they survive with this strange dour man for a master? With an almost helpless woman for a mistress? And two small children to look after?

The girls wore long dark dresses that reached to the floor. Tituba thought they looked like little old women, shriveled up with age, as they sat hunched over, shivering in the horrid damp of the closed-up cabin they all shared.

In spite of the cold, the master had them working on samplers.

When the master was out of the cabin, Tituba helped Betsey with her sampler, finally finishing it for her. The child's hands were so cold she simply could not guide the needle.

Abigail asked her to finish her sampler, too. Tituba refused, saying, "You're older than Betsey. You must finish it yourself."

The moment the master entered the cabin, Abigail said, "Tituba worked Betsey's sampler for her. Betsey didn't do it."

The master began to shout, "This is cheating, this is cheating—"

Mistress Parris sat up, weak as she was. Tituba moved towards her to support her, and the master turned towards the bunk, too. The mistress whispered, "Samuel, Samuel, there is no need to shout. It is too cold for a child to work a sampler. It is too cold—" and slumped down, exhausted. After her whispered protest there was no further mention of samplers.

They ate and they slept, and Tituba nursed the sick woman. If the sun was out, she and the children walked on the deck to get a breath of fresh air. The air was so cold they did not stay outside very long. The master moved his writing box into the captain's quarters and sat there and wrote out his sermons. Tituba thought the small cabin seemed warmer and bigger without him.

Whenever she and John met outside on the deck, they talked about the Parris family.

Tituba said, "I think the mistress will be better once we get off this rocking-back-and-forth ship. But I don't think she'll ever be strong. Betsey, the little one, is like her mother—not too strong. But Abigail, the niece, she's a strong one. She's a sly one, too. She's been through my bundle just as neat as can be."

"How do you know?"

"She didn't put the things back the way I had them."

"How do you know it was Abigail?"

"Because she was in the cabin when I discovered somebody had been in my bundle, and she got up and left, even though the ship was rocking and she's afraid to go on deck when the ship rocks like that. But she got up and went outside, and when she finally came back in, soaked from the salt spray, she wouldn't look at me. It was Abigail all right. I don't know what she thought she'd find."

Tituba kept the thunderstone wrapped in layers of cloth tucked inside the front of her dress. Sometimes at night she touched it, comforted by the thought that it had come from the island. As long as she kept it with her, she would have a part of the island with her. The old man who had given it to her had told her that if she ever thought her life was in danger, she was to unwrap the thunderstone and hold it in her hand. If she felt it move in her hand, it was a sign that she would live. She wasn't sure that she believed this, but she wouldn't want to lose the thunderstone.

She did not want to ask John when they would reach their destination. But after days of rough seas, cold winds, and the same weevily bread and the salt beef that left a queer unswallowable taste in her mouth, she said, "John, when will we get on land again?"

"If the weather holds good, we'll be in Boston before the week is out."

"Boston?"

"It's a big city. It's a big port. All the ships from England and the West Indies land there. The mate says you've never seen such a sight as the wharf there in Boston." His voice changed, and she knew he was quoting exactly what the mate had said and that the mate's voice was higher in pitch than John's.

"The ships come and go. They unload spices and silks and molasses and sugar. They ship out horses to the West Indies and they ship out fish, dried cod and herring. And they ship out timber. Sometimes a slaver pulls in with just a few slaves left aboard, and the fine rich ladies of Boston go down to pick one out. And the rich Boston merchants come down to watch the unloading, and some of them have a king's ransom in gold coins in their money boxes. They ship out and they ship in there on the wharf in Boston, and it's a rare sight to see."

Though she knew he was only telling her what the mate had said, she thought he sounded as though he had forgotten the island. She told him they must keep Barbados alive in their minds. After that, whenever she met him on the deck, she asked him if he remembered the color of the water, how blue it was, and the color of the sky, as blue as the water. She would name the trees that grew in the hills, and talk about the fruit and the fish—and then would suddenly stop, overcome by a dreadful homesickness.

The farther north they went, the more violent the winds, the rougher the seas, the colder the air. In spite of the cold, she ate her evening meal on the deck—a piece of the hard dry bread and the salt beef—standing, feet and body braced against the wind, chewing and chewing in order to soften up the bread and the beef so she could swallow. She couldn't help thinking how greatly this food differed from that produced in the island. The manny-manny tree produced an abundance of tender, succulent breadlike fruit. If you had a manny-manny tree, you'd never go hungry—certainly you'd never have to eat such bricklike food as this.

One night, as she stood there on deck chewing, she stopped eating and blinked, not believing her eyes. She peered and peered, felt a scream rising in her throat, and forced herself to swallow it and to keep looking to make certain she wasn't seeing a vision. A head was slowly emerging from a longboat that was stowed alongside the cabin. A head, and then the shoulders, and then the body of a boy—well, a half-grown young man. He was a big fellow. Though the light was fading, she could see that he had bright red hair and an impudent kind of face.

Then he saw her looking at him. He leaped on her so suddenly that he took her breath away. She thrust him away from her with a vigorous push, and he jumped at her again, trying to put his hard hands across her mouth to keep her from screaming.

She was breathless, panting, and finally she managed to gasp, "Stop it. What do you want?"

He watched her warily, obviously prepared to jump on her again. He said, "I'm starving."

"Here," she said, and held out a piece of the hard dry bread. He ate it so fast that she wondered he didn't choke on it. She handed him the piece of bread from which she'd taken a bite, and the salt beef. He hesitated. She said, "Go on, take it. I've eaten all I want. Are you a stowaway?"

He nodded and kept chewing. Then he swallowed, swallowed hard again to force what must be hard lumps of bread and beef down his gullet. "I came from London on a ship, all safe and secret," he said. "I thought the ship was headed for the Bay Colony. That's where I wanted to go. Instead I landed in Bridgetown. So I hung around the dock until I found a ship going to Boston, and I hid on board. I ate all my fodder days ago, and I've got to have food or I'll die."

"What's your name?"

"Pim," he said, and he shivered suddenly and his teeth chattered. "Could you get me something to drink?"

There was gruel in the cabin. The mistress never ate it all; she always left half of it. Tituba thought, I could bring him that, and if I can get hold of John, he could get water for the boy.

"I'll bring you something," she said. "I'll knock three times against the side of the boat. That means it's safe to sit up."

She found John and told him about Pim, persuaded him to get water and more of the hard dry substance that served as bread. Though she explained this was for a stowaway, she didn't tell him where the stowaway was hiding. John didn't ask. They both knew he talked too much; he told things without meaning to. He liked to talk to people; he tried to entertain them and amuse them, and he could mimic them—the exact tone, the lift of the eyebrow, the movement of the hands, and the speech—word for word exactly what they had said, whether it was a man or a woman or a child. Once he started doing this, he didn't sort out in his mind what he was to repeat and what he was to keep silent about. Because he had this strange gift, he simply went on repeating what a person had said.

John brought food and a blanket from the cook, explaining that the cook said he was glad to know there was a stowaway aboard and that he hoped he reached Boston without being discovered. Somebody ought to be able to get something for nothing from the miserable owners of this miserable brig. John leaned backward slightly, so that he looked fat like the cook. He had his arms akimbo, placed squarely on his fat hips, and he pursed his lips slightly, and from the way he held his head down a little and thrust forward, he seemed to have a double chin. He said, " 'Take the poor stowaway boy a good supply of salt beef, and plenty of water, John. Give him my blessing.' " He chuckled. " 'The brig is called the *Blessing*. We'll make it a blessing in deed as well as name.' "

Every night Tituba took food to Pim, the stowaway. The night before they were to land in Boston, she looked around the deck carefully and cautiously before she knocked on the side of the longboat where he was concealed.

She handed him bread and salt beef, saying, "We'll be in Boston tomorrow. Good-bye and good luck to you."

"Thank you."

She turned away from him quickly, feeling that someone was watching. She thought she caught a glimpse of Abigail's long dark skirt. But she wasn't certain. Betsey would have been afraid to go on deck at this hour. It had to be the bright-eyed Abigail.

When she entered the cabin the mistress was asleep, her breathing barely discernible. Though Betsey was in bed, she was still awake. Tituba thought how strange it would be to live in a place where it was so cold that you went to bed with more clothes on than you wore during the day. Betsey wore a nightcap, and there were two quilts and a heavy blanket on the bunk, and she still looked pinched and cold. Abigail was knitting, head bent over her work with an intense air, as though she were thinking of her knitting and nothing else, and working at it very hard so that it would be perfect.

Tituba thought, I don't believe she's been sitting there all the while. She's been on deck. She touched one of Abigail's hands—it was icy cold. She touched her hair—it was damp, as though she had been standing somewhere where the salt spray could hit her.

"Come," she said, "it's time you were in bed. We will be in Boston tomorrow."

Chapter 2

DURING THE night Tituba could have sworn that the motion of the brig changed and that it was going around in circles, and up and down as well. The master groaned in his sleep, and once he cried out as though he were in pain. Betsey's breathing was heavy, and she snored as though she were a fat old woman who had something wrong with her throat or her lungs. The mistress was restless; she turned over and sighed, and called to Tituba in her gentle whispering voice, asking for water.

Tituba awakened early, aware that the sounds in the brig had changed. There was the sound of hurried movement. Someone banged on the door of the cabin, saying they would dock later in the day.

It was a sour kind of afternoon. Cold, rainy, and a gale blowing. But the air had a different smell. It had a land smell—even in the cabin. They had to stay inside until the *Blessing* was tied up at the wharf.

Tituba saw little of the wonder of the Long Wharf in Boston. She caught glimpses of other ships, saw piles of goods being loaded, but the rain was like a gray veil, and she could only catch glimpses through it of warehouses and of men moving hastily, trying to rescue goods that were perishable.

She took one little girl by each hand. John carried the small trunks and boxes off the boat, and the Reverend Parris half carried the mistress, supporting her awkwardly. Tituba paused for a moment and looked back; there seemed to be a sudden increase in movement on the deck of the *Blessing*. She stood still for a moment, watching. Two sailors had the redheaded boy, Pim, by the arm, and they were shaking him, and then the captain arrived, and there seemed to be more confusion and movement.

"They found the stowaway," Abigail said, blue eyes sparkling. "I told the captain where he was hiding."

"What will they do to him?" Tituba asked John, thinking, So Abigail *was* on the deck last night and knew where Pim was hiding.

John shrugged. "Find him a master with a strong arm."

"What are you talking about?" Reverend Parris asked.

"They found a stowaway on the brig, master," John said.

"I hope they whip him soundly. Dreadful thing to steal passage on a vessel. Dreadful. Like stealing a man's land or his house or his cattle or his money. Come along now or we'll be drenched. I've hired a cart. Don't keep the man waiting."

Tituba thought, That boy simply wanted to go from one place to another. I helped him by feeding him and I would do it again. But the master thinks of him as a thief who stole from his betters and who should be whipped.

The master was making hurry-up sounds, clucking almost like a hen, in his effort to get them to the cart he'd hired.

Tituba paused long enough to look back again toward the *Blessing*. The boy was being hustled along the deck. The ship bobbed up and down at anchor, and then there was a heavy gust of wind. Rain descended like a curtain, cutting off the view and obscuring the redheaded boy, the *Blessing*, the Long Wharf.

Tituba tightened the shawl around her head. This was a cold rain. She shivered in spite of the heavy cloak and the warm shawl. John loaded their boxes and bundles into the cart the master had hired. The mistress and the two children got into the cart. Tituba and John and the master walked alongside it. The street was paved with cobblestones. There were houses and shops built right up to the edge of the street. Some of the buildings were stone, some brick, but most of them were wood.

Fortunately they didn't have to go very far from the wharf, and the master knew the way, but they were thoroughly soaked by the time they reached the small house where they were to live. Then they stood in the street, in the rain, waiting while the master went to the house next door to get the key.

It was a wrought-iron key, and Tituba thought it looked big enough to open the door of a castle, instead of this little two-story frame building. Inside it was very dark and very cold. It smelled of dampness and of smoke. There were two small rooms in the front and a large kitchen, or keeping room, which extended across the back. All three rooms had fireplaces. The largest one was in the keeping room, and there were settles on each side of it. There were no fires in the fireplaces.

The mistress said, "A cold bare hearth in this weather."

"There is no wood," John said accusingly to the master.

"We'll have to buy it," the master said. "Carts go through the town selling firewood. I don't know whether, in this rain—" He stopped and frowned, listening. There were footsteps overhead. It sounded as though two people were running and skipping, and then the sound quickened as though they were dancing.

"Where are the children?" the master asked.

Almost as if in reply there was the sound of footsteps running down the stairs, and Abigail and Betsey burst into the room, cheeks flushed, eyes sparkling.

"You should see upstairs," Abigail said excitedly. "It's all one great big room, with a big fireplace in it."

"What were you doing up there?" the master said severely. "I rented only the first floor of this house. You have no right on the second floor. It sounded as though you were dancing. If I thought you had been dancing, I would thrash both of you."

"We ran around the room, Uncle Parris," Abigail said meekly and looked down at the floor. "We were trying to keep warm."

"And dry ourselves off," Betsey said.

Someone pounded on the front door. Thieves, robbers? Tituba thought. Was it safe to open a door in Boston? Getting dark. Cold stormy night. Did the Indians ever attack right in the city?

"Tituba, answer the door," the master said.

She opened the door just wide enough to be able to see out, aware that John was standing close behind her.

"I'm Samuel Conklin, the weaver from next door, ma'am. I've brought ye some wood."

He was a tall man, slightly stooped in the shoulders. His hair was beginning to turn gray. He had his arms loaded with wood. When he saw John he said, "We'll build ye a fire first, and then ye come next door with me and get ye enough wood to last a few days."

John and Samuel Conklin built big fires in the fireplaces. Tituba draped their heavy, wet outer clothing in front of the fire in the keeping room to dry out. As soon as it was warm inside, they got the mistress comfortably settled in bed. It had been decided that one of the small rooms would serve as bedroom for the master, the mistress, and the two girls. The other small room would serve as the master's study. John and Tituba would sleep curled up on the settles in the keeping room.

The next day John went into the woods outside the city to cut wood. Samuel Conklin made an arrangement with a man who owned a horse and cart. John was to cut a load of wood for the master and haul it in the cart; then he was to cut a load of wood for the owner of the cart.

He came back, excited, and with a wondering look in his eyes. "I've never seen such woods," he said. "They go for miles. You could cut wood in there forever and never use it all up. All kinds of trees—big ones—the man with me said they were oak and hemlock, and there's a cedar forest and there are all kinds of birds. In some places there are so many trees that it is dark—daylight doesn't reach in. Some of the trees are so big and so old, they made me feel like praying."

Day after day he cut wood. A load for the owner. A load for the master. He kept piling wood up outside the kitchen until Tituba protested, saying, "You must be trying to supply wood for the whole of Boston. Or do you plan to sell it?"

"No," John said. "The men that work around the wharf say the winters are fierce. Snow and ice and wind, and so cold that your bones feel like they have frozen. There'll be weeks and weeks when I can't cut wood, so I have to build the woodpile so high it'll last for months."

Tituba hoped they wouldn't need all that wood, that the master would soon find a church, and then they would have a house that had more room in it. He said a church always supplied the minister with a place to live. He wanted a church in Boston. He felt that the people needed instruction. Boston had become a wicked city, a heathen city. He said that in many ways it resembled Babylon.

It surprised her that, feeling this way, he should have so quickly hired out John to a tavern-keeper. The tavern was near the Long Wharf, and there was a great deal of drinking and much sinful behavior. She supposed the master was in desperate need of money and perhaps the silver coins he received every week in payment for John's time there were so important to him it didn't matter how the coins were earned.

John said the work wasn't really hard. But it was woman's work. He brought in firewood and kept huge roaring fires in the fireplaces; he cleaned pewter and swept the floor in the tap room and sanded it, and chopped wood, and did some cooking, and made up beds with fresh linen.

Sometimes at night, in the keeping room, where they slept, he on one narrow wooden settle and she on the other, he fumed about his job.

"Kitchenmaid's work. Cleaning up after sailors and ship's captains and mates and whatever the sea casts up in Boston, with their earrings in their ears and their long greasy hair in a braid down their backs, and the mistress says, 'Ah, John, the captain in the front, take him a hot toddy. And the captain in the back room upstairs wants kill-devil with hot water. And the captain and his lady in the front room upstairs—' " He broke off and snorted. "Lady! You should see 'the lady'—a brazen hussy walking around barefooted in her shift."

He got up, imitated a woman's walk, mincing along, swaying his hips. " 'Make the fire blaze, John,' " he said in a woman's voice, " 'make a big fire so I' "—here he tittered—" 'so I won't get a chill, John Indian.' And the captain thinks this is funny and he laughs and then they both laugh."

He sat down on the settle, close to the fire, staring into it, "It's not a man's work. Not a man's work."

One night when he came home he was very upset. Witch Glover had been hanged that morning. He went to the hanging. Everybody went. They even closed the tavern.

He sat with his head in his hands. Just the two of them were in the keeping room. The master and mistress and the children were asleep in the little room that served as their bedroom.

"It was horrible," John said. "She wasn't anything but an old crazy woman. And they hanged her. Horrible. Then afterwards they all came into the tavern, so many they couldn't even sit down. And they drank rum and laughed and said, 'A hanging is thirsty work.'"

"What had she done?" Tituba asked.

"They said she witched the Godwin children. Just before she died she said hanging her wouldn't cure them. You should have seen the crowd of people gawking at her—an old woman, dirty, crazy. They said the black man stood by and whispered in her ear before she was hanged."

"Why did you go?" she asked sharply, not liking to see him so upset and wondering what he meant by "the black man." She hesitated to ask any more questions, and was angered with herself for not asking.

"I didn't know what was going on. They said, 'Let's go watch the Witch Glover. Come on, everybody. We'll have some sport. Come on, John Indian, come and have some sport.' I didn't know it was a hanging."

It was weeks before he mentioned it again. Sometimes when he sat silent, staring into the fire, she wondered if he was remembering the hanging of the Witch Glover.

Meanwhile, they settled into the little house as best they could. When the weather was fine, she took the little girls down to the wharf with her to buy fish. It was an exciting place. The wharf reached out into the open sea, and the boats could pull right up to it to dock. There were warehouses and countinghouses and shops and places where auctions were held, all along one side. There were wharves and small docks, all along the edge of the city, and places where they dried fish on frames, and then alongside there might be a bakeshop and a tavern, so that as you walked along you smelled fish, and the smell of the sea, and the smell of bread baking, and the smell of rum.

The mistress didn't like these trips. She had all the fears that an invalid has. They would get lost. They would fall in the water and drown. ("Don't go near the Long Wharf.") They would go into the woods and be attacked by fierce animals—wolves or bears or wildcats—that inhabited the untracked forest that stretched for miles outside of Boston. ("Don't go near the woods.") She warned them about the danger of fires, of being trampled by horses, teased and tormented by foreign sailors, chased by dogs.

At last Tituba said, "Mistress, if we waited until we thought it was safe, we would never go outside the house."

"I wish you wouldn't," she said. "I mean—I wish you wouldn't go unless John is with you."

"In that case, we would never go out," Tituba said gently. "He is at the tavern all day, and a good part of the night." She tucked the covers in around the mistress a little more tightly. "It's perfectly safe," she said. "Betsey is on one side of me, and Abigail is on the other. We hold each other's hands."

Betsey's grip on her hand was always tight—it was a frightened little hand. Sometimes the grip tightened beyond belief, and Tituba was sure the child was thinking: bears, wolves, wildcats, foreign sailors, big fierce dogs, angry cows, maddened pigs, stampeding horses.

Abigail's curiosity overcame any fear she had. She chatted as they walked along, head up in the air, asking questions.

"Why do all these boys wear leather breeches?"

"They're apprentices. Leather is tough, and they won't wear out their breeches as fast as though they were made of cloth."

"What is that dreadful smell?"—pointed little nose indicating that it was a very bad smell.

"Someone is boiling fat for soap-making."

"Is that man with the beautiful coat a lord?"

"Perhaps. Perhaps he's the governor of the Colony."

There was one place along the way where Betsey's hand always tightened in hers, squeezing it until it hurt. This happened when they came to the dooryard where there was a bear kept on a chain. Someone had tried to train him to do tricks. All he ever learned to do was stand on his hind legs and go around in a circle. The sight never failed to alarm Betsey. At first she tried to get them to run past this spot, but Tituba said no, they'd just attract attention and dogs would run after them, and some of those impudent bound boys would probably join the chase and set other dogs on them. It was best to walk past the bear, going at their usual pace. Betsey could walk on the side away from the bear and close her eyes so she couldn't see him. Once the child walked almost home with her eyes closed because Tituba forgot to tell her to open them.

Tituba kept hoping that the master would be called to a church. But the weeks slipped by and none of the churches in Boston asked him to be the minister. Then towards the end of November, five farmers from Salem Village came to see him and asked him to serve as pastor in their church.

After they left, Tituba heard the master tell the mistress that he had gone to Harvard College and therefore he wanted a church in Boston and nowhere else. When she told John about this, he said the talk in the tavern was that the Boston churches did not want the master because he had an invalid wife, that a parson's wife had to do a great deal to help him, and that a parson with two slaves was unusual—his family would be a costly one to support.

They spent the winter in the little house in Boston while the master waited to be called to a church. It was so cold that Tituba thought she would die. Wind and snow and sleet. She and the little girls could no longer go for walks. Once they had ventured near the Long Wharf, and it was like being out in the middle of the ocean in a ship in a violent storm. The water was gray-black, furious. Shutters banged and clattered; boats at anchor bobbed up and down, and some of them pulled loose.

Samuel Conklin, the next-door neighbor, suggested that Tituba learn to spin. "Helps pass the time in winter, and there's never enough good strong thread in Boston."

He introduced Tituba to Goodwife Trumbull, one of his neighbors. Goody Trumbull taught Tituba how to spin a thread on the flax wheel and on the wool wheel.

Tituba learned quickly. At first she was clumsy, breaking the thread, making it too thick. After a few days of practice she could spin a thread on the flax wheel so fine, so strong that Goody Trumbull said it was like magic.

"Looks like magic," she kept saying. "Looks like it

hadn't been made by human hands." She looked at Tituba slantwise, out of the corner of her eyes, as she said it.

Tituba smiled and pretended she thought this was very high praise and said, "Thank you kindly."

After that she spun a thread that broke easily, that was thick in some places and too thin in others, just like Goody Trumbull's thread.

Chapter 3

THAT FIRST winter in Boston, Tituba thought all the plants and trees were dead. She didn't say this to anyone. She mourned for them in silence. She could not imagine what it would be like to live where there were no green plants, no trees.

Samuel Conklin, the weaver who lived next door, said that spring would come and there would be green leaves everywhere—on trees and shrubs and all the little plants. There would be flowers and fruit and vegetables. "You wait and see."

She did not want to say that she did not believe him. She nodded and said nothing. He had come to ask the master if he could teach her to weave, and the master was out when he came, so he sat by the fire in the keeping room, waiting for him to return. It was Betsey who started talking about all the dead trees and plants.

When the master returned he brought cold air into the room with him. He stamped his feet, rubbed his hands together, and stood in front of the fire, warming himself before he took off his greatcoat and his woolen cap. He cut off the heat of the fire from the weaver and from the children.

The weaver stood up and talked to him, standing in front of the fire, too. He said, "I need a helper. I had one of those fiendish bound boys and he's run off. I'd like to teach Tituba to weave. She's got good hands for weaving and spinning."

"What are you offering in return?" the master asked.

"Good woolen cloth?"

The master shook his head. "No," he said. "We need money more than cloth. It will have to be coins. Come, we'll discuss it in my study. Is there a fire in there, Tituba?"

"No, master. It is laid and I will light it." She did not remind him that he had said it was a waste of wood to keep a fire going when he was not in the room.

She did not know how many coins the weaver paid for her services. But every afternoon she sat in his snug warm room, learning how to weave, how to thread the loom, how to work out a pattern. To her own surprise, she enjoyed it. He kept roaring fires going in his fireplace. After two hours of work he'd bring her a dish of boiling hot tea. Every day he said the same thing, "Helps keep out the chill. Come, sit by the fire and drink your tea."

He laced his own tea with rum. He drank it slowly; and then, having wiped his mouth with the back of his hand, he would add another log to the fire and go back to work.

At first her arms and shoulders ached from leaning forward and pushing the shuttle back and forth, back and forth. Once she became accustomed to this motion, she found she could work very fast.

She stayed at the weaver's until the light began to fail. She left reluctantly. When she reached the street outside, she pulled her shawl tight around her head and neck and hurried to get inside the master's dreary little house. It always seemed cold in the house, and so before she unwrapped her shawl, she poked the fire, added another log, drew the curtains, hoping to make this draughty keeping room feel like the weaver's big warm room.

One afternoon the weaver had a big order to fill, and she was later than usual when she returned to the little house next door.

The voice of the mistress, faint, querulous, came from the front of the house. "Tituba, is that you? Bring me a drink of the herb tea. I am faint for the want of it."

Abigail said petulantly, "I thought you weren't ever coming back. Where were you?"

Betsey said, "Titibee, Titibee, I'm so glad to see thee," and hugged her.

Tituba returned the hug and said to Abigail, "Why didn't you fix some of the herb tea for your Aunt Parris?"

"I didn't know how. Besides you should have done it."

"I can not be in two places at once, miss."

"You could if you were a witch," she said angrily.

Tituba boxed her ears soundly, hands cupped, striking the child's ears very hard. Abigail's cap fell off, and she shrieked, making a hideous sound that filled the room. Tituba shook her and said, "You stop that."

Betsey cried out, "Oh, don't," and clapped her hands tightly over her own ears.

There was a thud from the small front room where the mistress lay in bed. Tituba said, "She's fallen out of bed," and hurried into the room, Abigail and Betsey following close behind her. The mistress was lying on the floor.

"I tried to get out of bed. All that uproar—" she said. "I'm all right. It's just that my legs wouldn't hold me up. What happened?"

Tituba said, "I boxed Abigail's ears for being saucy."

Abigail helped Tituba get the mistress back in bed. Tituba shook her finger under Abigail's nose, "You behave yourself, or I'll box your ears even harder." It was best to say this now in front of the mistress so that if the mistress thought it was wrong she could say so.

The mistress closed her eyes, whispered, "Be a good girl, Abigail."

In the keeping room, Tituba took a small wooden box from the mantel and opened it. "The leaves are in here, Abigail. You get hot water and the small iron pot and put this much of the leaves"—she held a pinch between her fingers—"in the pot. Pour on the hot water. Let it steep and then strain it through this cloth. And take it to your Aunt Parris."

She didn't think the herb tea did the mistress much good. Mistress Parris had had a fever all winter; her cheeks were flushed, her eyes bright and shiny, her strength almost completely gone. Perhaps when the weather got warmer, if it ever did in this frozen country, Tituba could find roots or herbs in the woods that might help the mistress get stronger.

In the meantime, she had made an enemy of the nine-year-old Abigail. She could tell by the sullen expression on the child's face, by the way the bright blue eyes tried to stare her down. It was almost as though she could hear what went on in the child's mind—you boxed my ears, some day I'll box yours. You hurt me, some day I'll hurt you.

She finally accepted the fact that Abigail was her enemy, and though young, a dangerous enemy. On the other hand, Samuel Conklin, the weaver, was her friend, and though a new friend, a very good friend.

Towards the end of the winter, he came to see the master. He spoke forthrightly and directly, right in front of Abigail and Betsey, and within hearing of the mistress. Her door was open, and the weaver stood up straight and tall in the middle of the keeping room.

He said, "Mr. Parris, your Tituba only needs a little more practice to be better at weaving than me. She's got good hands. 'Tisn't easy to get that kind of weaver in Boston. Ye want to sell her?"

"Oh, no," the master said. "I got Tituba and John at a great bargain. I used almost the last of my money to buy them. Their owner had to sell them in a hurry to pay a gambling debt."

"I'd pay ye more than ye paid for her. I'd expect to."

"Oh, no," he said again. "With an invalid wife and my little daughter and my orphaned niece to be looked after, why I need more servants than other men. I couldn't sell Tituba. I would never sell her. She does everything in the house and nurses my sick wife, too—"

Tituba put her hand over her own mouth so her anger would not come out in the form of rude words. She could see Mistress Susanna Endicott in the house in Bridgetown, kneeling down in front of the great carved chest that stood at the foot of the vast bedstead, sobbing, "You were my jewels. You were my jewels." Soft white hands covered with rings and a jeweled necklace fastened at her round throat. She sold us, not her rings or her necklaces, but her human jewels. She gambled us away. And cried about it afterwards. They were the tears of the man-eating crocodile, moaning and crying to attract his victim and then eating the victim, tears still streaming out of his eyes as he chewed and swallowed. She decided she would not tell John about this, not until she could tell it without anger.

The weaver inquired gently for Mistress Parris. He said, "With the coming of spring, she'll feel better. Spring's on its way. Ye can feel it and smell it."

Tituba wondered if he knew what he was talking about. It was just as cold now in the middle of March as it had been in January. That night when John came home from the tavern she asked him whether he thought spring was on its way, and he said yes, the ice was breaking up in the harbor. The folk who came to the tavern said it was a sure sign that winter was over.

He said, "I've been able to get home every night this week. I couldn't have fought my way through some of those drifts before."

She nodded in agreement. The weather had changed. There had been an abatement of the wind that had blown all during the winter. She no longer awakened at night, jarred out of sleep by the sound of the wind in the chimney, a roaring sound that made her think she was in Barbados on the plantation where she grew up. When she was finally thoroughly awake, she found she was panting as though she'd been running, the dream so real that she thought she'd been working with the cane cutters in the sugar-cane fields and that a storm had arisen, one of those tropical storms with violent winds, and that the full brunt of the wind was almost upon them and the order had gone out, "Hurry cane, hurry cane," and it meant they had to hurry the cane out of the fields before it was ruined.

These dreams were so vivid that she was always surprised and shocked and disappointed to find that she was not in Barbados but that she was huddled on the hard wooden settle in her new master's kitchen in the little house in Boston. The wind made a howling in the chimney, and the fire had died down until it was only a glow of embers at the back of the fireplace. She would get up shivering and pile on wood, and then gradually the room would get warmer, and finally it would be so hot in front of the fireplace that she had to move away from the fire.

Sometimes when the wind roared in the chimney like that, her dreams about Barbados were so vivid that she thought she could smell the sweet smell of the crushed cane as it was being cooked. She'd never before had dreams that included odors—places and people and all kinds of happenings, but not smells. When she awakened she would sniff the air, and there was never anything even resembling the smell of boiling cane. There was the slightly smoky smell of the room and the smell of dampness that was characteristic of all the houses near the waterfront.

But all she said aloud to John was, "When spring comes I'll be able to go in the woods and look for plants and herbs."

"Maybe along the edges. It's not safe to go deep into the woods. There's Indians and there's wild animals—"

"You sound like the mistress," she said, amused.

It was six weeks or more before she went along the edge of the woods, looking for herbs. Spring came slowly to Boston. First the wind abated. Then the snow and ice began to melt. The days were longer. One day at noon it was warm enough, so that she could go out without her shawl fastened tightly around her head and shoulders.

People walking past the little house no longer hurried by, bent over, bundled up against the wind. The trees and shrubs that had looked as though they were dead and that had been dark silhouettes against the whiteness of the snow began to acquire pale-green, delicate-looking leaves.

Some days it was still very cold, but the water in the harbor was no longer a dark ominous gray. It looked greenish-blue, and the waves were tipped with white, and the water sparkled in the sun. She heard birds singing and knew they were nesting.

Even the harbor came alive again. She took the children to the Long Wharf to watch the boats come in and go out, their sails billowing in the brisk offshore wind.

There was enough daylight late in the afternoon, so that she could walk along the edge of the woods, basket over her arm, as she searched for herbs, for the roots of plants. She was certain she would find plants like the ones she had known in Barbados. She had to find something to give the mistress for her cough was worse.

Each afternoon she came back with an empty basket. She was sorely tempted to go deeper and deeper into the woods. But John kept warning her about Indians, saying that they were red devils who would scalp her and then kill her, that they were always at war with each other and with these new white settlers. So she simply contented herself with poking about the roots of trees with a long stick.

Late one afternoon she looked up, surprised to find a young woman watching her curiously. She had dark eyes that sparkled and a rosy complexion. She was wearing a black silk hood and a long full cloak of a dark red material.

"What are you looking for?" she said.

Tituba explained about her sick mistress, about the roots and herbs that grew in Barbados, and that she hoped to find them here in the woods near Boston.

The woman said, "I don't know what grows in Barbados, but I can show you what I gather here in these woods. Come." She turned directly into the heavily forested area.

Tituba hung back, "I don't think it's safe to go in there, mistress."

"I'm not going in very far. Nothing will hurt us. The Indians no longer come this close to Boston. And I've never seen any wolves or bears at the edge of the woods."

"Yes, mistress," she said.

"My name is Judah White."

Tituba bowed. "I am called Tituba," she said.

After that they met on the edge of the woods whenever the weather was fine. They came back from the woods with their baskets laden with the roots of plants, with the leaves, with the flowers. Tituba tied the herbs in bundles and hung them from the beams in the keeping room. It wasn't a big room, and she sometimes thought it looked like a simpler's shop she'd seen in Bridgetown. People came from miles to buy the cures that the simpler recommended.

Judah brought her a bundle of iris roots. She told her to brew them just as though she were brewing tea—to cut off thin slices of the root, cover it with boiling water, and let it sit until all the rich healing quality of the iris had gone into the water. She suggested that Tituba give this to her sick mistress and said it would stop the sharp pain she had in her chest and it would help the dreadful cough that left her so exhausted.

One afternoon when they came out of the woods with their baskets filled with the roots of lily of the valley, they saw ahead of them the Reverend Parris. He was walking slowly along the trodden path at the edge of the woods. The unexpected sight of his tall, thin, black-clad figure made a chill run down Tituba's spine. She shivered, just the way she did on a winter's morning when her bare hand touched the iron latch on the front door of the little house where they lived.

Judah glanced at her curiously, then slowed her pace to match Tituba's. "Do you know that man?" she asked.

"He is my master, the Reverend Samuel Parris."

"I've been looking for you, Tituba," the master said, as soon as he came abreast of them. "Your mistress needs some of your new tea to quiet her pain."

Judah nodded to Mr. Parris and went swiftly down the trodden path. Her long full cloak brushed against the weeds and the tall grass that bordered the path. Tituba thought there was something loving in the way the cloak brushed against the grass. She smiled thinking that if the grass were a cat it would be singing. Other people said that cats purred but Tituba felt that they sang.

"Who is that woman?" the master asked, watching Judah's swift progress down the path.

"Her name is Judah White, master."

"Judah White!" he said. He turned and stared at Tituba. "How do you come to know her?"

"I met her at the edge of the woods one day. Ever since then we've been going after herbs and roots. She heals the sick with the brews she makes."

"That woman is a witch. Never go into the woods or anywhere else with her." He looked past Tituba, and he said, "Where did she go? Where is she now?" His voice increased in volume. "She's vanished," he said. There was a note of fear in his voice.

Tituba turned and looked, too. The trodden path ran straight as a crow flies for a long distance. Judah was nowhere in sight. Tituba thought she saw the dark red cloak disappearing behind the trunk of a tree, but she was not certain.

"Master," she said timidly. "Why did you say that Judah White is a witch?"

"She came here from the Isle of Jersey where she is known to be a witch. The Boston clergy have been warned about her. Now come along, your mistress needs you."

He continued as he strode along. "It is by virtue of evil spirits that witches do what they do. None of them do good. If a witch does good, it is only that she may do hurt." He turned and faced her, saying emphatically,

"There is a law in the Colony that says, 'If any man or woman be a witch, they shall be put to death.' "

Tituba walked a little behind him, thinking about the iris roots from which she made the tea that soothed the mistress's cough and quieted her pain and helped her digest her food. Judah White had given her those dark-brown roots—the color of the earth on the outside, but inside they were white. When Tituba cut thin even slices from the root it gave off a faint but lovely fragrance. She was certain that only a good woman would bring so precious a gift.

Chapter 4

THAT SPRING the farmers from Salem Village came to see the master again. There were five of them— big men who wore clumsy boots and had heavy callused hands. Tituba noticed their hands when they removed their woolen caps. They nodded to her and said, "How-d'ye-do, mum," when she asked them to come in.

They left a barnyard smell behind them—a smell that lingered in the keeping room long after they were gone and made Abigail turn her pointed little nose up in the air and say, "Ugh!"

Afterwards the master sat by the fire in the keeping room. He bent forward, scowling at the fire, his chin resting on one of his thin hands.

Tituba wondered what he saw when he stared at the fire. She thought, I always see Bridgetown; the sun is shining and the fishing boats are going out. Did he see Barbados? What did he see? Surely not heaven, because he frowned so.

The next day the master made a trip to Salem Village. He borrowed a mare from Mr. Conklin, the weaver. He was gone for three days.

Tituba searched her mind for a way to describe what the little house was like without the master. The rooms seemed bigger and more filled with light. There was the merry sound of laughter and the brisk sound of people moving around freely, not on tiptoe. Betsey and Abigail laughed and talked as much and as loudly as they pleased. They ran and skipped and played games. The mistress smiled at their lighthearted play.

After the children and the mistress had gone to bed, Tituba told John that Mistress Susanna Endicott had sold them to pay a gambling debt. It seemed a good time to tell him this. They were sitting by a brisk fire in the fireplace in the keeping room. She felt free to speak out loud, not whispering or speaking in a hushed voice as she would have done if the master had been there.

John's face clouded, and he frowned. Then he shook his head, saying, "There is no need to cry about it now. It is like milk that was spilt. You can't pour it back again."

Suddenly he laughed. He said, "You were always reading those fortunetelling cards for Mistress Endicott. Why didn't you see this in the cards?"

"I don't know. Sometimes I could see things that were going to happen and sometimes I couldn't."

There was an exclamation of surprise from the doorway of the room where the mistress slept. Abigail came into the keeping room. She stood in front of Tituba, staring at her. "You can tell fortunes?" she asked.

Tituba hesitated. She said reluctantly, "My mistress, the one in Barbados, liked to have her fortune told. She sent me to a gypsy woman who lived near the bay in Bridgetown. The gypsy woman taught me how to read cards."

"Will you tell my fortune?"

She shook her head. "I have no cards. Besides I have not done that for so long I have probably forgotten how."

"Can you read palms?" Abigail asked, holding her hand out towards Tituba.

Tituba said, "No, I can't." She stood up and said briskly, "Best not get in the habit of being wakeful at night. Come, I will tuck the covers around you."

She wondered if she should ask Abigail not to tell the master that she could tell fortunes and decided that it was better to say nothing. It didn't really matter.

When the master returned, he was dispirited, out of sorts. Tituba half expected Abigail to say, "Uncle Parris, Tituba is a fortuneteller!" But she seemed to have forgotten about it; at least she did not mention it.

While the master warmed his thin hands in front of the fire in the bedroom, he described Salem Village. "It's just a village," he said unhappily. "It used to be called Salem Farms. I doubt that four hundred people live there. They are mostly farmers and fishermen. The farms are very far apart."

"I thought Salem was a busy port like Boston," the mistress said.

"Salem Town is a busy port. But Salem Village is very small. It's a separate village with its own meetinghouse. Salem and Salem Village are distinct and separate one from the other."

"Will you accept the offer to be their minister, Samuel?" the mistress asked.

"If they will agree to my terms," he said slowly. "It's not what I wanted—"

Later Tituba heard him reading aloud to the mistress. She listened to the rise and fall of his harsh voice and frowned. He was reading a list of the things he wanted from the farmers in Salem Village. He was to own the parsonage. The congregation would supply him with firewood. He was to be paid partly in money, partly in provisions.

The mistress said in her faint, whispering voice, "You think they will agree, Samuel?"

The master said, "Certainly. They have had trouble with all their ministers. They are a stiff-necked people and they can not get any one else. I am better qualified than the ones they've had. In the end, they will agree to my terms . . ."

That night Tituba told John what the master was asking—he would own the parsonage; he would have his firewood supplied.

John shook his head, "The talk in the tavern is that he'd better take the Salem Village Church. Whether they agree to what he asks or not. They say he won't get another offer any time soon. Folk don't like him."

Then John said, "You remember Pim, the boy that was stowed away on the boat with us? Well, he had to go to sea with the captain of the *Blessing* to work off his debt. The *Blessing* docked again this morning. The captain don't want him. The captain sold him to one of those farmers from Salem Village."

Tituba said, "They sell white people here in Boston?"

"Well, not really sold him. He's bound out. He'll be free when he's twenty-one. You should have seen him. The captain had him by the ear there in the tavern, and nobody would buy him or even bid on him. His red hair was against him. Some of the merchants who looked him over said he'd been marked by the devil with that carrot-colored hair. The man who got him from the captain of the ship didn't have to pay much for him."

Tituba shook her head in disapproval. "It doesn't seem right." Boy with red hair, thick curly hair, broad shoulders, big strong hands, lively eyes—boy like that sold to someone?

John said, "Oh, he won't mind. All those apprentices and bound boys and bound girls cheat the master, steal from the master, burn up his house, spoil his goods—and then finally run away. Not many of them stay till they're twenty-one. From the way Pim glared at the captain and the cool way he stared at the man who bought him—he won't stay with that man until he's twenty-one. His new owner is Deacon Ingersoll—he runs the ordinary in Salem Village."

Tituba poked the fire, sighed, said, "That's a woman's work—work in a tavern. It's not fit for a man or for a boy."

The master made another three-day trip to Salem Village. While he was gone, Tituba found herself singing or humming under her breath when she was working. She told stories to the children. She sat outside in the dooryard with a child on each side of her, Betsey leaning against her, warm, relaxed, Abigail sitting up straight, a little way off. She talked about the island—how the water felt warm, caressing when you swam in it; how delicious the fruit was, picked right off the trees; how they cooked outdoors behind the house; how the kitchen faced the bay, so that even during a storm it was like having a picture in front of you every day, a picture that changed—just a glance out of the window and you saw a new picture.

Here in Boston you couldn't see out of the windows in winter. They were so covered with frost it was like a curtain suspended in front of the glass, on the outside. She pointed out that now that summer was here, you still couldn't see the street clearly. The glass was a bluish-green and filled with places that looked like bubbles. It made everything in the street look as though it were underwater, in a place where there was a strong current and a great many air bubbles in the water so you couldn't see through it.

When the master returned, he said he didn't know whether he wanted to be the minister in Salem Village. Some of the people in the parish had told him bluntly they thought the requests he had made were unusual. He summed up his feeling about them by saying, "They seem an ungodly people."

Though his return put an end to all outward signs of merriment, it did not diminish Tituba's joyous response to this season of warmth. The weaver's big room was even pleasanter in summer than it was in winter. It had been warm and cozy in the winter; it was cool in summer. He had the back door opened wide, and there were small gardens on each side of the walk behind his house. There wasn't much land, but it was very carefully cultivated. She had never seen one patch of ground made to yield so much.

Every afternoon she worked in the weaver's garden,

hoeing, weeding, for the sheer pleasure of it. He gave her vegetables when they ripened—string beans and peas, and, later in the season, corn and carrots and turnips and pumpkins.

Even the master, who mostly ignored what he ate, spoke of how tasty the meals were now that there were fresh vegetables.

It seemed to her that she had barely become accustomed to the warmth, to the pleasure of stepping outdoors without bundling up in shawls and heavy cloaks, when the days began to shorten and it was cool after the sun went down.

Then one evening in early September when she came back from the weaver's, she found the master and the mistress and the children quite excited. The farmers from Salem Village had called again, and this time they had hired the Reverend Samuel Parris. It seemed to her that the smell of barnyards lingered in the keeping room.

The mistress was sitting up in bed, smiling and talking to the master and to the children.

"We'll have our own house and there will be plenty of room," he said.

"Is it a big house?" Abigail asked.

Betsey said, "Will I have a room all my own?"

Tituba said, "When will we leave? How long will it take to get there?"

"We leave in November. It will take us all day to get there."

"Is it a big house, Uncle Parris?" Abigail asked again impatiently.

"Well, yes. But more important than that, it will be ours. We will own it."

"We'll own the house, Samuel?" the mistress asked doubtfully.

"Yes," he said briskly. "They've agreed to it. Those five farmers who came the last time agreed to it. I'm to have my firewood, and two thirds of the salary will be in provisions and one third will be in cash. I will have a deed to the parish house and land. It's a very good arrangement."

"I never knew a parish to deed the parsonage to the minister," the mistress said.

"That's what these people have done. The paper I drew up reads that 'we will give to Mr. Parris our ministry house and barn, that and two acres of land next adjoining to the house.' I'm to be their minister for the rest of my life. Because it says, 'that Mr. Parris take office among us, and live and die in the work of the ministry among us.'"

Tituba thought he sounded as though he were reading from the Scriptures; his voice had slowed and taken on a note of solemnity. He said, "Let us pray," and she felt as though he thought he was already in the meetinghouse in Salem Village.

September, October, November—it seemed no time at all, and the air had turned cold again; the water in Boston Harbor no longer sparkled—it had a dull grayish look, and on some days it was almost black—and the wind blew harder and harder. During those three months the mistress and the two little girls talked unceasingly of Salem Village and the parsonage they were to occupy. Tituba said little about it—she agreed that no matter what the parsonage in Salem Village was like, it would be better than the first floor of this tiny house in Boston, a cramped place to live and a noisy one, too. When the doors and windows were open they could hear all the sounds of the street, and they were so close to the wharf that there was a great deal of coming and going past their door.

This would be the third move she'd made—the first one from the cane fields to the home of Mistress Susanna Endicott in Bridgetown, Barbados, and then from Bridgetown to Boston, and now from Boston to Salem Village.

They left Boston on the fifteenth of November, 1689. They had the loan of three saddle horses; their bundles and boxes followed in a cart. John supported the mistress in front of him; Abigail rode on a pillion behind her Uncle Parris; and Tituba held Betsey in front of her. Tituba wrapped the shawl around both of them; close together like that, they were both warm. She thought, she's six years old now, but what a small, light-boned creature she is—like a kitten.

After they left the outskirts of Boston she found herself glancing back at the mistress. True, John was big and strong, and had strong arms and broad shoulders, so that the mistress could lean back against him, but it seemed like a long difficult journey for a sick woman and a tiring one for two little girls. She had suggested that the master hold Abigail in front of him, much as John was holding the mistress, and just as she was holding little Betsey. But he said, no, his arms would get too tired, and he had to hold the reins, and the mare he was riding seemed excitable.

Tituba started to say, "But the child's arms are going to

get very tired—" and then bit her lower lip hard to remind herself not to argue with her master.

They entered the same heavily wooded area in which
she so often had gathered the roots and leaves of plants
and herbs, following a trail worn by horses' feet. She
thought with regret of the friends she was leaving—Samuel Conklin, the weaver, and Judah White, the woman
she had been forbidden to see again. They went deeper
and deeper into the woods. There was an ominous darkness and heaviness about the forest. But it was not silent.
Birds flew up with loud squawks and cries of alarm; sometimes there was a loud crashing sound as though a tree had
fallen, and then a different sound of branches breaking as
though their passage had disturbed some large animal,
which was blundering hurriedly through the under-
growth. She listened, strained to hear—was the animal
going away or coming towards them? Always overlaying
these sounds was the jingle of harness and bit, and the
sounds the horses made—occasional neighing if they
halted, the snorts and blown-out breath if the pace increased.

They rode through miles and miles of forest. There
were great stands of pine trees, junipers, cedar, hemlocks,
oaks. Tituba was surprised whenever they came upon an
open meadow with tall grass and no trees. Sometimes the
sunlight sparkled on a small cove or an inlet. When they
found a fresh-water stream, they watered the horses, and
they all got down and walked about, stretched their legs,
and Tituba gave everybody pieces of johnnycake and salt
beef.

Mounting again, they proceeded in the same order with

the Reverend Samuel Parris heading the procession. He said they were going north and a little to the east.

Tituba was aware that for most of the route they were near water; they kept coming to little inlets and tiny coves, brooks and small ponds, and sometimes the open sea. Though the horses were mares trained to be ridden, they were held to a jog, jog, jog that Tituba found painfully slow. But the trodden path was rough and uneven, and the sick woman would have been dreadfully jolted by a faster pace.

They passed clearings where there were farmhouses and barns and smaller outbuildings and salt meadows. The houses were far apart, a mile in between, two miles, sometimes three miles. The master knew who owned some of the big tracts of land. He called their names, but they meant nothing to Tituba—she hoped they would soon arrive at their destination. By the time the sun was directly overhead the mistress was so white and wan that it frightened Tituba to look at her whenever they paused to rest or water the horses.

The sun was low in the sky when the master reined in his horse again. "We're almost there," he said. "This is the meetinghouse."

They had come to a clearing in the forest. The meetinghouse stood in the center of it. There were no trees near it. It was a large wooden building equipped with heavy shutters that could be closed over the small windows. A big stone in front of the door served as doorstep. Propped up against the outside of the building was a great timber. It was so huge that Tituba decided it must have been hewn from a very old tree.

"That timber was left there after the meetinghouse was built eighteen years ago. No one has ever bothered to move it. These farmers are a shiftless lot," the master said.

Picking up the reins, he said, "Just beyond here where the path curves you can see Deacon Ingersoll's ordinary. We will be riding past it. But we must hurry along for it will soon be dark."

They jogged along for another mile. They came to a cleared area and he drew up his horse. "There," he said with a wave of his hand. "There's our new home—the parsonage!"

They looked at the house in silence. It was a big house, perhaps three times the size of the house they had lived in in Boston. Tituba frowned. She tried to estimate the amount of cleared land—perhaps five acres? There was a barn behind the house, so she could have cows and chickens and geese and start collecting down for a feather tick, and they could have a horse—enough cleared land so the animals could graze—why then was she dismayed? It was the sight of the house that alarmed her. It had a forbidding, desolate air, and if she could have refused to enter, she would have done so. The front door sagged on its hinges; the path leading to the door was overgrown with weeds.

The master got down from his horse, and Abigail jumped down unassisted. The master helped little Betsey to the ground, held his hand for Tituba, and then Tituba and he helped the mistress to the ground. She could just manage to stand up as they supported her under the arms, and then John jumped down from his horse and picked her up. They all headed towards the house, Tituba leading the way. Just as she reached the big stones that served as steps, she stopped.

"What's the trouble, Tituba? You're blocking the path," the master said.

Tituba pointed to the stone steps. "Look!" she said. On the topmost step, centered in front of the door, right in the middle of the step, placed as carefully as if the space inside had been measured, were two hen's eggs.

The master smiled, and the mistress said in her gentle, whispering voice, "Someone has brought us two fresh eggs."

Tituba said, "I don't think they're fresh."

A heavy fetid odor hung in the air. Even the master must have smelled it, insensitive as he was or appeared to be to smells and sounds. He sniffed twice and looked towards the woods and said, "What is that dreadful smell?"

Nobody answered him. Abigail said curiously, "Tituba, why don't you think the eggs are fresh?"

Before Tituba could reply, the front door opened. A rosy-cheeked, smiling woman, brisk in speech and in manner, stood in the doorway.

"Well, now, ye must be the Reverend Samuel Parris," she said. "Welcome to the Village and to the parsonage. I'm Sister Mary Sibley—I live across the way, not too far from the meetinghouse. I've got fires going in all the fireplaces. It's nice and warm inside. This time of year it don't take much of a fire to take the chill off."

Tituba could tell that the master wasn't pleased to find that the first and only parishioner to greet him was a woman, especially one who talked so easily and so fast.

He said stiffly, "This is my wife, and this is Elizabeth,

my daughter, and Abigail, my orphan niece. This is Tituba and this is John—my servants."

She wondered why he didn't say "My slaves"—perhaps farmers didn't have many slaves, and he thought it might not be a good idea to say that he owned two slaves.

Mary Sibley said, "Oh, the poor dear," looking at Mrs. Parris. "We'll put her right to bed and we'll get her something hot to drink and then something to eat. I've got hot fish stew in the big iron pot. It's a good thing there are bedframes and feather ticks in the parsonage." She started out the door toward Mrs. Parris, glanced down at the step, and saw the eggs. She was silent for a moment. Then she looked around uneasily, "Wherever did they come from—"

The master said, "I never knew fresh eggs to cause so much comment, Goodwife Sibley—"

Mary Sibley said, "Fresh eggs, indeed!" and pushed them off the steps into the path. She took a stick and broke them. The master said, "What are you doing?"

"You still think they're fresh?" she said. The smell was rank and foul, "Old and rotten," she said sharply, "and may the Lord preserve us from such evil."

"Yes," Tituba said softly, under her breath.

Chapter 5

GOODWIFE SIBLEY helped Tituba get the mistress settled in bed in an upstairs room. It was a low-ceilinged room, almost as long as it was wide. There were three small windows, but the room was dark inside because the small-paned windows didn't let in much light. It was partly furnished. At least there was a bedframe with a feather tick on it. The bedframe was supported by sturdy posts that reached almost to the ceiling. And there were two stools, one on each side of the fireplace.

Before they left the room, Goody Sibley stood back away from the bed and examined the mistress as carefully as though she were a doctor, studying and appraising the thin body, barely discernible under the quilt, staring at the gauntness of the face—the cheekbones showing, the skin so deathly white that the long lashes looked black as fireplace soot against that whiteness.

She said disapprovingly, "Most folks use the downstairs parlor to sleep in. All the other pastors slept downstairs."

The mistress said, "Mr. Parris has to have a room to himself to work in and write his sermons in." Her eyes stayed closed, and Mary Sibley had to bend forward in order to understand what the soft whispering voice was saying.

Tituba and Mary Sibley left the room together. As Tituba followed her down the narrow staircase she thought, Steep stairs, narrow treads, abrupt turn near the top of the stairs. If you went up or down them too fast, you could stumble and break your neck. It was like going down a ship's ladder.

Mary Sibley kept talking, even on the way downstairs. "Folks have already sent ye in food. There's apples and onions and carrots. Ye've got salt fish and salt beef and turnips and dried apples. Some's in the keeping room and some's in the lean-to in the back."

The keeping room was a big, low-ceilinged room with smoke-darkened rafters. A huge summer beam ran the whole length of the room, and because the ceiling was low, Tituba felt as though the great beam was pressing down on top of her head. The fireplace was big enough to roast a whole ox in. There were settles on each side of the fireplace, long enough so that she could stretch out full length though John was so tall he'd have to bend his legs when he was bedded down there.

Mary Sibley said, "Folks will send ye eggs and butter. This be farm country, and ye'll always have corn meal and salt pork and the fisherfolk will send ye fresh fish."

Tituba nodded, and kept looking around. Goody Sibley knew how to build fires. This one was burning steadily and quietly. There was a big backlog and smaller, long-lasting logs on top of it. The room smelled like all the houses she'd been in in the Colony—smell of smoke and smell of dampness. The floor and the hearth had been swept.

She was surprised to see that there was a loom, a big one, in one corner of the room. There was a flax wheel, a carding wheel, and a winding wheel.

Mary Sibley said, "I see ye looking at the loom. It don't work, but the wheels for making thread still work. They belonged to Mistress Burroughs, the wife of one of our pastors. When she died, the Reverend Burroughs left the Village in a hurry and left all this behind him."

Abigail ran into the room, shouting, "The cart's come. The cart's come."

"Hush!" Tituba said. "Quiet yourself, and then go and help unload the cart."

Abigail and Betsey set to work to help the driver unload the cart. They brought in small cooking pots and two stools.

Mary Sibley took advantage of their absence from the room to question Tituba.

"What is wrong with Mistress Parris?" she asked.

"She has a weakness in her chest. The cold and the dampness make it worse."

"Is she always in bed?"

"No. When the weather is cold she coughs a great deal and this weakens her. Then she has to stay in bed." During the past winter the mistress had never once left that little room off the keeping room in the house in Boston. During the summer she was able to sit outdoors. But the first bit of cold weather had set her to shivering and coughing.

"It makes a lot of work to have a sick woman upstairs.

Ye'll be carrying food, carrying wood." Goody Sibley shook her head. "Where did ye come from?"

"Boston."

"Lived there long—did ye?"

"Almost a year."

"Ah," she said, and her breath came out in a sigh, and her eyes glistened with excitement. She ignored the presence of the children. They had just come into the kitchen, lugging a small chest. They set it down with a thud because it was heavy and slipped out of their grasp.

Sister Sibley said, "They hanged the Witch Glover in Boston. Did ye see it?"

Tituba shook her head. John had seen it. When he had finally got so he could talk about it, he said it looked as though everyone in Boston, everyone in Massachusetts, everyone in the whole Colony had seen the hanging. There were so many people crowded together that you couldn't move, could hardly breathe. If you'd taken a deep breath, your ribs would have pushed against somebody else's ribs. All of them come for miles and miles through woods and forests, down small streams in boats, to see an old woman hang—a wild-looking, snarling creature. Tituba said none of this to Mary Sibley; she simply shook her head to indicate that she wasn't there.

Abigail said primly, "The witch had overlooked the Goodwin children with her evil eyes. The Goodwin children screamed, and cried out, and said she was freezing them and boiling them and sticking pins in them. Their tongues were pulled way out. Way out like this," said Abigail, sticking her tongue out so far that Tituba scowled at her, angered at all this sudden talk of witchcraft and witches. Mary Sibley, a grown woman who should know better, was excited, her face flushed. Abigail's bright blue eyes were gleaming with excitement, just like Mary Sibley's.

Goodwife Sibley nodded, "Indeed, yes. And before they hanged her she told them that hanging her wouldn't cure the children. And it didn't. She'd put a spell on them and nobody could take it off. They said she bartered her soul to the black man. That's how she got her power over the Goodwin children."

Then she said softly, thoughtfully, "We've got some here might be witches, too. Right here in the Village. Everywhere ye go, ye find them. The folks' cows sicken and die or they won't give milk or the pigs go mad or the butter won't come—usually a witch has overlooked them. Some of the witches have cats as familiars. The devil gives them the cats to serve them and do their bidding."

Her glance slid around Tituba, and Tituba remembered the neighbor woman in Boston who had taught her to spin, and who ran her finger along the thread, and spoke of how strong it was and how smooth and how quickly made, "Just like magic." Something in her glance had warned Tituba not to spin thread like that any more, at least not where Goodwife Trumbull would see it. Mary Sibley's sliding-around glance reminded her of the eggs on the doorstep, rotten eggs, on the parson's doorstep. Everyone knows what that means, she thought, somebody trying to bewitch them, to cast a spell on them. On the minister? On Tituba? If it was Tituba—why Tituba?

Mary Sibley said, "Where'd ye come from before ye was in Boston?"

"Bridgetown, Barbados. It's an island in the West Indies."

"Ye be the minister's servants? Ye and John?"

"We be his slaves," she said simply. "He bought us in Barbados before he came to Boston."

"Slaves," Mary Sibley said. "The parson has two slaves and a sickly wife. Did the committee that hired him know he had a sickly wife?"

The conversation was interrupted by the master. He entered the keeping room from a back door, opening it with an abruptness that startled the women and the children—he seemed to burst into the room.

"There is no wood," he said and his voice was harsh and loud. "I was promised my firewood. Where is it?"

Mary Sibley shook her head, "There must be a mistake, Mr. Parris. The minister supplies his own wood."

"It's written down," he said, growing more and more excited. "It's in the agreement. I'll unpack my papers and find it. The congregation is to provide me with firewood."

"No matter," she said calmly. "Ye'll need wood and ye'd better get started cutting some right away. Then ye can settle it with the committee that hired ye."

"It's written down," the master repeated.

"Perhaps it is. Meantime ye'd better cut wood. It will take plenty of wood to keep that upstairs fire going all the time." Then she said very deliberately, "With sickness in the family it's easier if the sick person is downstairs."

The master's thin face flushed. Tituba left them there to argue about it and went outside, found John, told him there was no wood and he would have to cut wood right away before it got dark.

She paused to look at the house and see whether her first impression of it had been right. Sometimes if she stood still, used all her senses, sight and sound and touch and smell would make a place speak to her. She closed her eyes and took a deep breath. She decided it was not an evil house. It was sad and gloomy. Nothing about it suggested happiness in the future. It had been a long time since anyone had been happy in this house. People leave something of themselves in a house, and the spirit of this house was frighteningly sad.

She could hear the rustle of leaves, a murmuring sound from the wind in the trees, and faintly the sound of the horses, a snorting, snuffling sound, and the jingle of harness as they moved, shifting position slightly. Something seemed to be moving about in the woods at the far side of the land; there was a rustling in the leaves, and it sounded as though twigs were being broken with a sharp, cracking sound. As she stood there she was certain that she smelled the same unpleasant odor that even the master had smelled when they were about to enter the house.

She walked all around the house. The wood had weathered to a deep dark brown. The windows were small with small panes of glass. They gave the house a sly look, as though the windows were half-closed eyes stealing glances at her, not wanting to be caught in the act of looking directly at her. All the windows needed washing. The chimneys were darkened by streaks of soot from the top all the way down to the roof, indicating the chimneys had been on fire more than once.

The paths from the house to the barn and from the

house to the well were overgrown with tall weeds. She bent over the well to look down into it—someone had thrown a dead animal in it, she could tell by the smell. Someone obviously didn't want them living here; she glanced at the house again—and shivered. Dark house, dark sky, winter coming on—she would have the care of two little girls and a sick woman. They would be living in this farm country, deep in the woods, far away from other families, and for all his cold harsh voice and his quick temper, the master was as helpless as a child—he would soon find work for John to do, work away from the house. This would bring him in a little income, but it would leave her with everything to do—fires to tend, and cooking to do, gardening, washing.

There was a place behind the house where someone must once have had a garden; she poked down into the ground with a stick. The soil was soft and pliable—it had been worked in—she would grow vegetables in it, and right near the door she could have flowers. There was a big barn so they could have one or two cows, and a mare so the master could call on the people on the farms a long way off.

She would look at the barn and then go back to the house. The back door of the house opened, and Betsey Parris came running out. "Wait, Tituba," she said, "wait for me."

They walked hand in hand towards the barn. Tituba said, "We'll have a cow and a horse in here, and when we come in the barn it will always seem warm because of the animals. It will be filled with the sound of their breathing and their talk sounds. We'll get hens and we'll get a strutty cock-rooster to keep the hens happy and order them around and to crow early in the morning."

They were about to go in the barn when she paused and said, "Close your eyes and I'll close mine and we'll pretend that the animals are already here—"

She closed her eyes, and then opened them. She stopped talking. The smell inside the barn was overpowering. It was dark in the interior, and she peered around, expecting to see someone inside. There was no one there.

Betsey squeezed her hand, and looked up at her. "Let's not stay here, Tituba. It don't smell good."

"You wait for me outside. I want to look around." But the child wouldn't let go of her hand. Tituba stayed long enough to see that someone had been sleeping in a pile of old musty hay in a corner of the barn. It was hollowed out into a nestlike shape. Someone had lived in the barn, had perhaps planned to spend the winter there and been angered when the Parrises had moved in.

She was certain that the occupant of the barn had placed those rotten eggs on the front doorstep of this house as a warning of trouble to come.

Chapter 6

THEY ATE heartily of the well-seasoned fish stew that Mary Sibley had prepared. It was so hot that steam came up from their trenchers, as they sat lined up on the settles. There was no table, so they held their trenchers in their hands as they ate.

The steam from the fish warmed the inside of Tituba's nostrils. She leaned back against the settle, looking at the others. The girls sat side by side. Betsey had eaten everything that had been served to her. Abigail had a second helping and was still eating hungrily, head bent over her food. John was still eating, too. He sat next to the master. The master had finished and was staring into the fire.

Mary Sibley said, "I'll be leaving ye now. I must be home before it's dark."

"Wait," the master said, "I want you to hear the words of the agreement I drew up."

He went into his study and came back with a neatly rolled paper. He stood in front of them, unrolled the paper, and began to read. Then he stopped, cleared his throat, said, "I should explain first that this says my salary is to be sixty pounds per year, one third in money and the rest in provisions. This is the exact wording:

" 'When money shall be more plenteous, the money part to be paid me shall accordingly be increased.

" 'Second, though corn or like provisions should arise to a higher price than you have set, yet, for my own family use, I shall have what is needful at the price now stated, and so if it fall lower.

" 'Third, the whole sixty pounds to be only from our inhabitants that are dwelling in our bounds, proportionable to what lands they have within the same.

" 'Fourth, no provision to be brought in without first asking whether needed, and myself to make choice of what, unless the person is unable to pay any sort but one.

" '*Fifth, firewood to be given in yearly, freely.*

" 'Sixth, two men to be chosen yearly to see that due payments be made.

" 'Seventh, contributions each Sabbath in papers; and only such as are in papers, and dwelling within our bounds, to be accounted a part of the sixty pounds.

" 'Eighth, as God shall please to bless the place so as to be able to pay higher than the sixty pounds, that then a proportionable increase be made. If God shall please, for our sins, to diminish the substance of said place, I will endeavor accordingly to bear such losses, by proportionable abatements of such as shall reasonably desire it.' "

There was silence in the room. Mary Sibley's expression was stubborn.

The master said, looking down at Goodwife Sibley, frowning at her, "You understood what I read? '*Firewood to be given in yearly, freely.*' There should have been a woodpile here."

"There could be a misunderstanding," she said agreeably. "In the church record book it says, 'the minister to find himself firewood.' But ye talk it over with the committee. Meantime, ye'd better get firewood piled near the house. The winters is fierce. I'll leave ye now before it gets dark. I'll come again tomorrow and bring my niece, Mary Walcott. She's older than your niece Abigail, but they'll enjoy to know each other."

She took a long, dark woolen cloak from a hook near the door, put it around her shoulders, then wrapped a shawl tight around her head and shoulders, and slipped quietly out the back door.

Tituba went upstairs to see to the mistress. She was asleep. She looked as though she hadn't changed her position since they got her into bed. Tituba pulled the quilt closer and higher around her shoulders, put another log on the fire, then went back downstairs, thinking of all the trips she would make up and down these steep ladder-like stairs, carrying wood, carrying food.

When she got downstairs, she sent the little girls up to bed. The door of the master's study was closed. She could hear him moving around inside the room—probably hunting for more papers and signatures to prove that the farmers of Salem Village were to provide their minister with wood. She sat down by the fire, and sat there so long and so quietly that a mouse came out of his hole and scampered across the floor.

John came in from outside and put a huge log on the fire. He said quietly, "It's an oak log. It'll burn all night once it gets going."

There was a soft, flickering yellow light in the immediate area of the fireplace. The rest of the room was so dark there didn't seem to be any corners. John sat down on one settle and she curled up on the other. They said nothing, waiting for the master to go to bed before they talked.

Finally the door to the study opened and the master came out. He had a lighted candle in his hand. He came into the keeping room to bid them good night. His body made a grotesque shadow on the wall—very tall, very stooped in the shoulder—and the hand that shielded the candle and the arm looked as long as a bedpost.

They waited until they heard his footsteps going up the stairs. Then John said, "What do you think?" He got up from the settle, put one of the stools directly in front of the fire, and sat down, his legs hunched up to his chin.

"Nobody has ever really liked this house," she said. "It's been years since anybody had a garden here or kept a cow. This isn't a good house." She waited for him to say something, and when he didn't, she said, "Someone's thrown dead animals down the well. Somebody's been living in the barn."

"Just neglected," he said easily. "It'll be all right. If somebody's been living in the barn, they probably got angered when they heard the master was going to live here and threw a dead rabbit or a dead squirrel down the well. I'll clean it out tomorrow. We'll get the place fixed up for winter. Plenty of wood. We'll need a mare and a cow. In the spring we'll get pigs. In a year or two we'll have a pleasant place here."

She didn't argue with him. He had probably heard a farmer talk this way. We'll get a mare. We'll get pigs. In a year or two everything will work out. She didn't believe it would ever be a pleasant place to live. The master was getting ready to fight with these farmers and fishermen who lived in Salem Village. There was only one of him and four hundred or more of them, counting their families in, too. They hadn't forgotten how long it took him to decide to come to the Village, all of nine months. He had made trips to the Village, and they had made trips to Boston. Some of them promised him one thing, and others promised him something else. She doubted they'd ever get it straightened out.

She closed her eyes and then opened them, studying the room in the firelight. The fire was burning quietly, no sparks, no smoke coming into the room. No sound inside the house. None outside either. Everything was still. Then slowly, slowly, as though an invisible hand were pushing it, the door of the minister's study opened. She sat up, hand over her mouth, so that no sound of a scream would come out, and made a violent motion to attract John's attention, and then pointed to the door.

John stood up, hands on hips, watching. No one came into the room. The door stayed open.

Tituba said, "Who opened the door? Did you see anyone?"

He shook his head. "Of course not. Doors in old houses often open by themselves. The floors slant and the latches don't hold. They get worn down, and—"

She said, "John, I don't like this house—"

"Hush," he said. "We have no choice. We have to stay here." He put his arms around her. "Remember the slave has no choice but to go with the master. But remember also the slave has to survive. We will survive."

His arms were strong; his shoulders were broad, and his

breath was sweet, and she went to sleep in his arms. The last thing he said to her was, "No matter what the master says about firewood, I'll see that there's plenty of it. Otherwise we will all freeze."

When she awakened in the morning, she was certain she was in Bridgetown, in Barbados, and that it was a beautiful warm morning. She jumped up quickly, thinking she would swim in the little inlet just beyond the house. Then she shook her head and a feeling of sadness came over her. There was a big roaring fire in the fireplace in the keeping room, and John was standing in front of it, rubbing his hands together, warming them. That meant it was cold outside, and he must have brought wood in and added a big log to the fire. He had already cooked mush in an iron pot. It was steaming over the fire.

He was laughing at her. "Where were you going? Looked as though you were going to run off somewhere in your sleep."

"I was in Bridgetown," she said. The master entered the keeping room, and she didn't add that she had been dreaming. He looked at her curiously. He was rubbing his hands, too, so it must be cold in the mistress' room upstairs, fire probably gone out.

She rebuilt the fire in the mistress' room, fed her, fed the children, swept the floor of the keeping room, and sanded it. If John could clean out the well and start building a woodpile, they would have water and she could cook. They would be able to keep warm until the master found out whether he was to provide his own firewood or whether the parish was to provide it.

The master came out of his study, said, "I am going to

see Deacon Ingersoll. We must straighten out the matter of firewood."

In the days that followed she had to admit that the master had been right about his need for a separate parlor or study. There were always committees composed of three or four men who met with him. He spent a great deal of time writing, keeping records, careful records of the provisions that were brought in, of the money that was paid him.

He started with a meeting late the next afternoon. Four men came to the house and sat with him in his study. They got into an argument. She could hear their voices through the door.

When the voices in the study were at their loudest and angriest, there was a knock at the front door. Tituba was sweeping the hearth; the girls, Betsey and Abigail, were behind the house, helping John build the woodpile. He had found an old sled behind the barn, and he had made sides for it, and by piling it with wood and hitching himself to it as though he were a horse, he could pull a big load of wood from the nearby woods to the house. The little girls helped him unload it and stack it, though they could only handle the smaller logs.

She opened the door and then stepped back away from it, frightened. She recognized the smell, the same smell that had been around the dooryard when they arrived, the smell that had been in the barn. This, then, was the person who had slept in the hay. At first glance she thought, This is an old woman with two heads. Both heads had matted, uncombed hair hanging down over their faces. She wondered what race of people had skin that was dark gray in color, and then she saw that the woman's skin was so dirty it looked gray rather than white.

The woman's clothing was ragged and torn—she looked literally like a bundle of rags. She said, "We're hungered, Dorcas and I. We're hungered."

The woman had a child on her back, strapped to her back the way the Indian women carried their children. The child looked to be about three years old. The child's head seen over the old woman's shoulder made her look as though she had two heads.

But she wasn't an old woman. She pushed Tituba aside with a quick, hard thrust of her arm and entered the house. She looked around the keeping room, looked at the fire, bent over the black pot that stood on the hearth. She moved with the speed and agility of a young, strong woman. The kitchen was filled with the sour, dreadful smell of her.

The master came out of his study and frowned when he saw the woman.

"What do you want?" he demanded.

Tituba thought the meeting had not gone well—he sounded cross.

"Food," she said. "Dorcas and I are hungered."

"Be off with you," he said harshly. "There is no excuse for beggars. Be gone before I take a stick to you."

Her eyes glittered under the matted hair. But she said nothing. She went out of the house, down the stone steps; as she reached the weed-covered path, she turned towards them and shook her fist and muttered something. Tituba could not understand what she said.

The men had come out of the master's study and were watching her.

The master told Tituba what their names were: Deacon Ingersoll, the tall man with the kind face; Sergeant Thomas Putnam, shorter, with a more severe expression; Captain Walcott, younger; and Marshal Herrick, a handsome man with a swaggering air. They were dressed very much alike. They all wore felt hats with broad brims that came down almost to their shoulders in back, and heavy shoes; they had swords at their sides and each man carried a musket. This surprised her. In Boston, men moved freely about the wharf and the streets without muskets.

When she mentioned this later to John he said that the farmers in the Village always carried their muskets with them, never beyond the reach of their hands, almost a part of their dress like their shoes, because there was always the danger of attack by the Indians. Many of them had taken part in the war against the Narragansett.

Deacon Ingersoll said, "That was Goody Good. If she comes again, feed her. It's better to feed her."

"Why?" the master asked.

"Because no one knows what it is she mutters when she goes away. Just now when she went down the path she was muttering to herself. She might work some mischief against you."

"Against the pastor?" the master said.

"Against the pastor or anyone else," he replied quietly.

"How?"

Deacon Ingersoll shrugged. "If she comes again—feed her. We all feed her and her children. It is better that way, believe me."

Then they were gone, too. Tituba left the doors open to air out the room, to rid it of the smell of Goody Good. It would be cooled off, but it would smell fresh like the keen, crisp fall air instead of vilely like Good.

She stepped outside. She would help John and the children bring in wood, help build the woodpile against those cold winter days.

She started to walk away from the house and stopped because stepping delicately around the side of the house, tail straight up in the air, came a young cat. As Tituba looked at him, he sat down, washed his face, cleaned his whiskers. She thought, Why that's a money cat, a good-luck cat. He was black and dark gray and yellow, though the yellow was almost orange. He was a short chunky cat, round-headed, nicely proportioned, and his fur had a very sleek look.

When he saw Tituba he walked over to her and brushed against her skirt, tail up in the air, walked around her, purring. She leaned over and stroked him. She would keep him. She would say nothing about him to anyone. She would simply keep a cat. If the master objected she'd say they had to have a cat because of the field mice—they'd soon be living in the house. The cat looked up at her and his eyes were huge—they looked as though they had no bottom—great, clear pools of light amber.

"Come, Puss," she said. He followed her into the house. She fished some tender bits of codfish out of the big black pot and put them in a shallow wooden bowl, near the hearth. He ate hungrily but very daintily, and occasionally he stopped to purr. After he finished eating, he mewed and scratched at the door. She let him out and didn't see him again until the next day.

The master was so upset about the firewood and the visit of the committee from the church, he hurried through the evening prayers. And then he told them to sit down by the fire while he read to them what the committee told him was in the church record book. He had made a copy of it:

"Eighteenth of June, 1689—it was agreed and voted by general concurrence, that, for Mr. Parris, his encouragement and settlement in the work of the ministry amongst us, we will give him sixty-six pounds for his yearly salary —one-third paid in money, the other two-thirds parts for provisions; and Mr. Parris to find himself firewood, and Mr. Parris to keep the ministry house in good repair; and that Mr. Parris shall also have the use of the ministry pasture, and the inhabitants to keep the fence in repair; and that we will keep up our contributions, and our inhabitants to put their money in papers, and this to continue as long as Mr. Parris continues in the work of the ministry amongst us, and all productions to be good and merchantable. And, if it please God to bless the inhabitants, we shall be willing to give more; and to expect, that if God shall diminish the estates of the people, that then Mr. Parris do abate of his salary according to proportion."

There was silence in the room when he finished. Betsey Parris, who had been staring at the fire, seemed to have gone to sleep; Abigail yawned openly and rubbed her eyes, though she knew these signs of boredom irritated her Uncle Parris. John put another log on the fire.

The master crumpled the paper in his hands. "This house is mine," he said. "They said it was to be mine. Now they say keep it in good repair as though it was still theirs. And they say, 'Mr. Parris to find himself firewood.' I was to have my firewood given to me."

John rearranged the logs. He glanced at the master and then looked away. Tituba moved towards Betsey. She was sitting on the settle and, though her eyes were open, she seemed to be asleep. Tituba bent over her, touched her gently on the wrist, and increased the pressure a little. The child stirred and sighed, and said something that Tituba couldn't understand.

"Best get the children to bed. Come, Betsey," she said firmly. Betsey shivered; then she stood up, and taking hold of Tituba's hand, they went towards the stairs. Abigail followed them.

Tituba glanced back over her shoulder at the master. He was staring into the fire, saying, " 'Mr. Parris to find himself firewood.' "

Chapter 7

I T WAS a month before Mary Sibley expressed approval of the size of the woodpile John built behind the minister's house. Day by day it grew bigger until it was a truly handsome structure, sweet-smelling, neatly arranged. The big backlogs for the keeping-room fireplace were stacked together, as were the smaller logs for the other fireplaces. Then there were sticks of hard wood to keep the fire going, and a pile of kindling—lightweight wood, twigs and chips that would burn quickly and easily if the fire needed freshening.

Mary Sibley came often to look at the woodpile. Every few days she would shake her head and say, "With a house this size and with a sick woman upstairs—most unusual to have a sick woman upstairs—ye'll need a pile of wood almost the size of the house. Ye'll have to be forever cutting wood just like a beaver, John Indian."

There was a month of good weather. During that month, John cut wood until as he said, "I'm chopping and sawing even in my sleep." But he found time to do other things, too. He repaired the barn roof, replaced the missing hinges on the barn door. He made new parts for the big loom. This was slow, tedious work. He stopped frequently to ask Tituba, "What is this part supposed to do?" Then later, "Does it do it now?" Before he finished repairing the loom he said, "Someone who knew how to use a loom fixed this one so it wouldn't work."

Sometimes when she was weaving she would try to envision the person—a spiteful man? a spiteful woman?—a bent-over figure, carefully wrecking the loom.

When Mary Sibley found that Tituba knew how to spin, she brought flax to be spun. She exclaimed over the fine, strong linen thread that Tituba produced on the flax wheel.

She said, "Tituba, if ye'll spin thread for me, I'll set the pastor up with hens and a cock."

So before the first snow, there were hens clucking about the barnyard, and there was a cock that crowed early in the morning. They had fresh eggs to eat. She cooked the first one for the mistress.

The hens enlivened the barnyard. Puss, the money cat, enlivened the dooryard, too. He grew fat and sleek and round. Betsey and Abigail fed him tidbits—choice portions of fish or beef. They stroked his fur, told him how handsome he was and how clean.

During the day, he sat outside near the back door. If Tituba came out to gather eggs or to bring in wood, he walked in and out under her long dark skirt, as though he were deliberately smoothing the fur on his back by letting the skirt brush over him gently. She talked to him, too, murmuring to him. When he looked up at her and blinked, she half expected him to answer her. His light brown eyes were green in the center—it was like looking into glass balls—only the color kept you from seeing all the way through them.

He was gone all night. Tituba had tried to keep him in the house, but he mewed and scratched at the door until she let him out. Late in the morning he would appear at the back door. He looked as though he had been in the very heart of the forest, in a far-off mysterious place, which he could not share with her. There were unspeakable secrets in his eyes, even his fur seemed to reject her hand.

"It will soon be so cold, Puss," she said to him reproachfully. "You will not roam through the forest at night. You will stay in the house and hug the hearth, as a cat should." She wrapped her shawl around her head and shoulders before she ventured outside early in the morning.

In the meantime they acquired a skittish brown mare and a placid brown-and-white cow. This meant the master could visit the outlying farms because he had a horse to ride, and the family would have milk. But they would lose John. For in exchange for the loan of the mare and the gift of the cow, John had been hired out to Deacon Ingersoll.

When John saw the animals he frowned. "What are we going to feed them?"

"We'll have hay and grain," the master said. He explained that he would ask the ratepayers to supply him— they were supposed to provide him with whatever he needed.

The farmers brought enough hay and grain to last through the winter months.

Tituba missed John during the day. The master was away from home a great deal. Even if he'd been there, he wasn't much help. He was better at reading and writing than he was at lifting heavy logs or carrying pails of water from a well. He couldn't even carry a bowl of gruel upstairs to the mistress without slopping it over, and his exclamations of distress and surprise when the hot gruel hit his hand only upset the mistress.

John came back to the parsonage at night. But he would only be able to do this while the weather was good. When the winter storms came, he would have to stay at Ingersoll's.

A week later the weather turned very cold and windy. Tituba let the little girls stay by the fire in the keeping room until John came back from Ingersoll's. When he came in, Puss came in with him, tail up in the air, purring when he saw Tituba, behaving exactly as though he were accustomed to spending the night in the keeping room. He sat in front of the fire and washed himself carefully.

"Tell us about Ingersoll's ordinary. What is it like?" Abigail asked.

John said that it was the biggest house in the village. The taproom, where people sat to eat and to drink cider and beer, was almost as big as the meetinghouse. Quite often church meetings were held in the taproom. He said that Deacon Ingersoll had a license to sell "beer and cider by the quart on the Lord's day." After morning service in the meetinghouse, the farmers and their families who came from a long distance came to the taproom to refresh themselves.

He said that you could get all the news of the Colony right there in Ingersoll's taproom. It stood on a curve in the road to Andover and Ipswich. Travelers from Boston who were going up into Maine and travelers from all places to the east of the Village stopped there to rest their horses, to eat and drink; some of them spent the night.

"You hear everything," he said. "Little pieces of gossip. Big important pieces of news. The farmers come there to trade with each other. You know who had a good onion crop and whose cornfield didn't yield. Fishermen come there to make arrangements to sell a big haul of cod or haddock."

Everybody worked, serving beer and cider and food. The fires had to be kept going; the hearths had to be swept; bread had to be baked; the bedrooms had to be cleaned.

John said, "Everybody works." Then he threw his head back and laughed, "Ha! Ha! Ha!"

They all looked at him, surprised. Abigail's eyes widened; Betsey blinked and said soberly, "Why are you laughing?"

John said, "Everybody works but that stowaway— Pim."

Abigail said, "Stowaway? What stowaway?"

"That redhead boy, Pim, who stole his passage on the ship we came in. The *Blessing*. Pim is at Ingersoll's. He's bound out to Deacon Ingersoll for seven years."

"Did you know he was on the ship?" Abigail asked.

Tituba got up, stood behind Abigail, looked hard at John, and shook her head.

John said, "In Boston they said he was a stowaway. They sold him to Deacon Ingersoll in the taproom of that tavern where I worked."

Abigail said, "He doesn't work?"

"He works some," John said carefully. Then he laughed again. "But not too much. He spills cider when he pours it. If he fixes a fire, a burning log will come rolling right out on the floor—beyond the hearth to the wooden floor. If he sweeps he sets up such clouds of dust and dirt and ashes that he sets everybody to choking and sneezing and coughing. If he brings in logs of wood for the fires, he falls down with them, and the wood lands on top of people who are eating or drinking. They box his ears. They call him clumsy. They shake him until his teeth rattle in his head—and he still spills things and falls down and breaks everything that's breakable." He paused and stared into the fire.

"Tell us some more," said Betsey.

"I'll tell you what the place looks like, and then I'll tell you this song that Pim sings, and then we'll all be off to bed." He was silent for a moment and then he said, "The house is big, and it's set back from the road. It faces to the south, so the sun comes in almost all day. And in front there is an open space; it's all flat and smooth and covered with grass, and there are no weeds. Deacon Ingersoll lets his sheep graze there, and they keep the grass cropped, and it's a pretty sight. They call that big open space in front Ingersoll's Common. Then off to the northeast, not far from the house, in sight of the house, is the blockhouse. They keep watch there against Indians. There's always somebody there, armed with a firelock. They keep watch day and night."

He stood up to indicate he had finished talking.

"Will you sing the song?" Abigail asked.

"Oh, yes." He threw his head back, put his hands on his hips, a big man obviously copying the mannerisms and manner of Pim. It was a merry tune, and the words were loud and clear, and he kept time with his foot.

> *"Let the world slide, let the world go;*
> *A fig for care, and a fig for woe!*
> *If I can't pay, why I can owe,*
> *And death makes equal the high and low."*

"Oh, John," Betsey said, eyes sparkling, "I didn't know you could sing like that."

Abigail clapped her hands together, softly. "Sing it again," she pleaded, "sing it again. I've never heard anything like it."

John looked questioningly at Tituba. She listened for a moment. There was no sound from the master's study, so he was probably sitting with the writing box open before him, head bent over, so absorbed in what he was writing that he was deaf to what was going on in the keeping room. Tituba nodded her head.

This time John either sang louder or the rhythmic sound of his foot hitting the floor disturbed the master. The study door opened just as John sang, "If I can't pay, why I can owe. . . ."

The master said, "What unseemly song is that?"

John said, "It is a very old song, master. One they sing in England."

"Where did you learn it?" he demanded.

"I heard it sung first in Boston in the tavern where you had me work, master. Since then I've heard it sung in Deacon Ingersoll's ordinary."

"Who sings it there?"

"Fishermen sing it there. I do not know their names, master. Men who come down from Boston sing it, too. I do not know their names either."

"It is an evil song. Do not sing it here." He glanced at the flushed faces of the little girls, their sparkling eyes. He said, "It is time for prayers and time you were in bed." He looked at the big fire in the fireplace and frowned, saying, "We can not afford to keep such big fires going. My wood is still not supplied to me." He motioned that they were to kneel and then knelt himself and prayed long and earnestly, his harsh voice rising and falling, now in supplication, now in admonition.

"Get to bed," he said when he had finished. He went back into his study and closed the door.

Betsey started obediently towards the stairs, but Abigail lingered behind. She said quietly to John, "You didn't tell him that Pim, the bound boy, sings that song. Why was that?"

John said, "Because slaves and bound people do not tell tales on each other."

"Why?"

"Because their lives are not their own. The people who own them do not protect them. No one protects them. And so they have to protect themselves and each other."

"What would happen to Pim? What were you protecting him from?"

"They would beat him—"

"It would be good for him," Abigail said pertly. "He drops things and breaks things on purpose. That's why you think it's funny. You laughed—"

Tituba said, "Miss, it's time for you and Betsey to get to bed. Step lively."

Tituba watched them as they left the room. Just recently Abigail had learned to make her long skirt express her feelings. Now she made it flounce around her feet and thus express her disdain for Tituba and her objection to being sent upstairs to sleep in a cold room, leaving the warmth of the hearth for Tituba and John. Betsey walked smoothly, and her long skirt moved smoothly, too.

Abigail had closed the door. The latch clicked shut noisily. Then Tituba sighed gently—glad that it was night and she could talk freely to John. The mistress was asleep; the girls were on their way to bed, and the master was shut up in his study. The keeping room was theirs. She sat near the fire on one of the settles, and the cat curled up at her feet. He seemed to stare into the dark corners of the room, for the firelight only reached a little way into the room. He turned his head as though he were watching something. From the way he moved his head the object he was watching was slowly emerging from the darkness that nearly obliterated the door of the minister's study. It made her uncomfortable for she couldn't see what he was looking at.

She said, "Come, Puss. Come!" stooped down and picked the cat up and held him on her lap, stroking his head, caressing him under his chin until he began to purr. She said to John, "Listen, he's singing. Just listen to him."

The master came out of his study, and the cat jumped down heavily with a thump. He crept under the settle directly across from Tituba. Only his nose, his whiskers, and his eyes were visible. His eyes looked enormous, without depth, no bottom, like looking into Boston harbor. He watched the master's approach with an unwinking gaze.

"Where'd that cat go?" the master asked. He bent over and looked at the cat and then straightened up hurriedly. "I don't like its looks. Get rid of it."

Tituba said firmly, "Master, we have to have a cat. There are rats in the barn. There are mice in the house. They are eating our food. We need a cat."

"I don't like cats. I never have liked them. Put it out."

She stood up, looked straight at him. A small woman sturdily built, her expression usually gentle, now defiant. "There are mice in the house, master," she said, deliberately repeating what she had said before just as though she were talking to six-year-old Betsey.

The master's eyes flashed with anger, and he lifted his arm as though he were going to strike her. John said, easily, "It's good to have a cat, master." He was in the shadows, leaning on the settle, watching them, his eyes narrowed to slits.

The master said, "Yes," and lowered his arm. He made a complicated business of lighting a candle, and then he went up the stairs to bed.

John said, in a low voice, "He's quick to anger because of the church meeting in Ingersoll's late this afternoon.

The master was there, and the deacons read him that same thing he read to us, where they had it written down that he was to keep this house and the pasture in good repair and get his own firewood. He knew that that meant they hadn't given him this house—he has no deed—and he won't get a deed."

"What happened?"

John made his voice sound like the master's. "He shouted at them, 'I never heard or knew anything of it. Neither can I or will I take up with it, or any part of it.'" And then John lowered his voice still further, "He was so angered that he said 'They were knaves and cheaters that entered it in the parish book.'"

Tituba said, "He said that to the church people?"

John said, "Yes. And a hush and a stillness came in Ingersoll's big room. The talk in the tavern is that he's greedy. He wants what isn't his. And they say he's mean-tempered. Lieutenant Nathaniel Putnam said to him, 'Sir, then there is only proposals on both sides and no agreement between you and the people.' And our master said, 'No more, there is not, for I am free from the people and the people free from me.' Then he left, and he slammed the door behind him, and the folk say it will be just like a war here. Some will be for him and some will be against him, and then they won't pay their rates, and the meeting-house will not be kept up, and there won't be enough to pay his salary."

Tituba shook her head—rotten eggs on the doorstep to greet them, a door that opens by itself, the general air of neglect, of gloom around and inside this house, that tramp woman named Goody Good who had walked down the weed-filled front path, her rags fluttering around her, turning to shake her fist, and muttering something—threats, inviting disaster.

"I wish the master had never come here."

John said, "No matter. The slave must survive." He opened the back door, and cold air rushed into the room.

"Close the door quickly," she said.

"I've got an oak backlog almost as long as the fireplace, almost as wide as a boat. I'm going to bring it in. It will last way along into the morning. When I knock, open the door for me."

He was covered with a light powdering of snow when he came back into the room. She watched him work the big log into the house by himself with handspikes. She thought, Winter is here; it is beginning to snow. I will be shut up in this house with the master and a sick mistress and two little girls. The house doesn't want us. The neighbors don't want us.

But it was warm in the keeping room. The words of Pim's song echoed in her mind, "Let the world slide, let the world go—"

Chapter 8

THE NEXT morning when John left for Ingersoll's the sun was shining. The money cat went out the door ahead of him. In the doorway the cat turned and gave Tituba a look of annoyance, as though she had fooled him into spending the night in the house when he could have been deep in the forest; she should have let him out of the house as soon as the snow stopped.

He lifted his feet daintily, leaving a clear track of his paw prints. Later Tituba traced his path through the snow. He had gone all the way around the house, had walked around the barn, and then gone towards the forest.

Soon afterwards, Mistress Anne Putnam, wife of Thomas Putnam, clerk of the church, came to see the mistress. She brought her daughter, Anne Putnam, Jr., and the Putnams' bound girl, Mercy Lewis, with her. Mistress Putnam was a tall, thin woman with flashing dark eyes. The daughter, Anne, Jr., was as thin and white-faced as the mother.

Mercy Lewis, the bound girl, was lively and rosy-cheeked. Her cap kept coming off her head, and a great mass of yellow hair the color of buttercups tumbled down over her face and shoulders.

Mistress Putnam spoke sharply to her, "Mercy, get your hair under your cap before Pastor comes into the room."

Mercy hastily tumbled her hair into place on top of her head and put on her white cap.

They all went up to the mistress' bedroom. The conversation made Tituba uneasy. Mistress Putnam said that her sister had died in this house. "But not in this room," she said, looking around. "We always keep sick people downstairs. She was married to Mr. Bayley who was the minister. Mr. Burroughs' wife died here, too. He was another of our ministers. He didn't pay for his wife's funeral —went off and left all his belongings. We had him arrested and brought back until we could get it straightened out."

Tituba found herself wondering, Was it Mr. Burroughs who had fixed the loom so it wouldn't work? Was his the bent-over figure she had visualized carefully wrecking it?

"Just before Mr. Parris came, there was Mr. Lawson—"

"Did his wife die here, too?" Abigail asked, interrupting her. "Tell us about it downstairs. We'd best be going down for Aunt Parris has to rest now." She said this in such a grown-up way that Mistress Putnam stared at her in surprise.

After Mistress Putnam's visit, Tituba found excuses for keeping other callers away from the mistress. She was afraid they, too, might talk about all the ministers' wives who had died in the ministry house.

Mary Sibley came often and brought her niece, Mary

Walcott, with her. Mary Walcott was an expert knitter. She taught Tituba how to knit the long woolen stockings they all wore. Goodwife Sibley made broths and puddings for the mistress. She had remedies for everything— for coughs and colds, for frost-bitten fingers, for headaches.

Before the winter snows closed the paths and roads, Tituba came to know many of the bound girls and boys and the slaves who belonged to the farmers in Salem Village. The farmers sent them to the house with provisions for the minister. When there was a knock at the door, late in the afternoon, she knew it would be Black Peter or Mary Black or Cindy, slaves who belonged on nearby farms. Or it might be one of the bound girls, Mary Warren or Elizabeth Hubbard or Mercy Lewis. They brought corn meal, salt beef, salt cod, onions.

By the middle of December, snow was piled up so high they could not see out of the windows. Tituba and the master dug a tunnel-like path to the barn so they could feed the animals. Tituba did most of the digging for the master tired easily. The woodpile dwindled, and Tituba began to wonder if it would last through the winter.

They were never really warm. The mistress shivered under the quilts and the blankets piled on the bed in the upstairs room. The little girls said they couldn't sleep it was so cold in their room. Tituba let them sleep on the settle in the keeping room where John used to sleep.

She missed John's visits, and so did the girls. He had brightened the early evening for them with stories and bits of news. He had made them laugh by imitating the speech and the gestures of the farmers and the fishermen.

Sometimes he put his hands on his hips and walked back and forth, nodding his head as he talked, copying the exact words and gestures of someone who had been in Ingersoll's taproom. He could transform himself into an old man, by bending over and putting his hand behind his ear to indicate that he couldn't hear very well. Or he would pretend to cough and clear his throat, so that you knew the person talking had a rheum in his throat or lungs.

Betsey and Abigail were bored and restless. Tituba, watching them and listening to them, understood exactly how they felt. She felt the same way. The days were so short that it seemed as though night set in soon after they had their noonday meal. She cooked and spun and wove and cleaned. The money cat stayed so close to the fire, his paws tucked under his chest, that she thought he'd singe his multicolored fur. The master shut himself up in his study, working on his sermons and his prayers.

It was so cold in the master's study that his ink froze in his inkstand. She could hear him stamp his feet and thought she could hear him rub his hands together—a dry sound that she disliked.

On the second of January the weather turned warmer. The snow began to melt—first it softened and then it actually melted. In the afternoon, the master said, "I shall take the mare and go visit the sick."

Tituba sat by the fire, spinning flax into linen thread.

Abigail said, "Tituba, now that Uncle Parris has gone out, tell us about Barbados," a note of command in her voice.

"No, miss. Not now. You put more wood on the mistress' fire upstairs. And Betsey, you carry some of the hot herb tea up to her."

"When we come downstairs, then will you tell us about Barbados?"

"We'll see—"

Abigail returned to the room first; she moved quickly with a self-assurance that suggested she was older than she was. Betsey followed close behind her. Tituba made no effort to conceal that thin, frail, awkward Betsey was her favorite. She gave her the lightest tasks, quite often held her in her arms and crooned to her as though she were a baby. Sometimes Betsey seemed to be dreaming, sitting with eyes half-closed. She forgot to answer if asked a question. She stayed quite close to Tituba, leaning against her if they sat on the settle, cuddling up to her as if for warmth and love.

"Now?" they said. "Now? Will you tell us about Barbados now?"

She nodded and stopped spinning. They all sat down at the trestle table and rested their arms on the table.

She started talking about the island rather slowly. Then she got up and walked up and down, talking faster and faster, gesturing as she talked, thinking that if she talked fast enough she could dispel this cold winter afternoon. She hoped to make it disappear—all of it: the gray, heavy sky, the white snow, gray-black trunks of trees, and the forest that surrounded them, ominous, endless—broken here and there by frozen coves and ponds and brooks— ice everywhere. So cold outside that if you took a sudden deep breath of the cold air it seemed to reach inside your lungs and all the moisture in your lungs turned to ice—even your eyeballs frozen, the tips of your fingers, your toes without any feeling, numbed by the cold.

She did not tell them that almost every night she dreamed her soul was in Barbados, that it went back there to be warmed by the sun and cooled by the trade wind. She did not tell them that when she awakened in the morning, she lay still without moving long enough to allow her soul to re-enter her body. She had discovered that if she was slightly chilly her dreams of Barbados would be more vivid. But the memory of these dreams lingered, and so she was able to make the girls see the island again. Their eyes followed her as she walked up and down.

Betsey said, "The island is yellow-white in the sun."

Abigail said, "It blazes in the sun; it is so yellow and the sunlight is so strong."

"The water is warm," Betsey said, "And I am swimming in it. In a little pool of blue water all my own. I haven't any clothes on. Nobody can see me."

"I smell the sugar cane. They are cooking the cane," Abigail said. She had her head thrown back, and her eyes were closed. She sniffed as though she really smelt something.

Tituba said, "There is the sweetish smell of rum and the bitter sharp smell of coffee. And the trade wind is blowing across the island. This wind blows all the time. So that you feel just right—not hot, not cold—just warm enough. You don't go wrapped in shawls and coats and capes. You just wear your dress and your turban to keep the sun from the top of your head. When it rains, it rains hard and then the people stay inside."

When they stayed inside, they told stories, long intricate stories. The stories got better the oftener they were told. There were people who told just one story, and everybody knew this, and would ask that person to tell his story about the monkey in the garden. The story improved with each telling.

They told these stories in the rainy season in the island. This was the snowy season in Salem Village and a very good time to tell a story. So Tituba started a story about the guppy man and the monkey, how the guppy man discovered that the monkey could talk to the dead. The monkey would call the guppy man in the middle of the night. "Guppy," she said, "Gupp-e-e-e-e-e. He would walk all around outside Guppy's house." She repeated the cry over and over, a monotonous rhythmical sound, "Gupp-e-e-e-e-e."

Then she stopped right in the middle of what she was saying because Abigail was staring hard at Betsey. Though Betsey was sitting at the table, she looked as if she were asleep, but her eyes were open. Her unwinking gaze was fixed on a pewter bowl that was filled with water. It had been left on the table. She was staring at it, not moving. She was breathing through her mouth, making a loud, sighing sound.

"Betsey," Tituba said.

Betsey muttered something unintelligible. "Betsey," she said again, firmly but gently.

Abigail shrieked, "Betsey!" and grabbed the child by the arm, shaking her.

Betsey screamed and burst into tears. Abigail said, "What was the matter with you? What were you doing?"

Tituba cradled Betsey in her arms. "Hush, now," she said. "You're all right. You're all right." She was such a thin little child, small for her years, delicately boned.

Abigail said, "What was the matter with her? What was she doing?"

Tituba shook her head, indicating that Abigail was to be silent. "She wasn't doing anything. She kept looking at that little bowl of water too long and she—well, she fell asleep."

"Her eyes were open. She wasn't really asleep. She was making a funny noise. People don't make noises like that when they're asleep. They snore like Uncle Parris"—and she made a loud snoring sound, almost a trumpeting, as she inhaled and then exhaled.

Betsey smiled, just a ghost of a smile. Tituba hugged her close as a reward.

Someone banged on the back door. Abigail opened it just a crack, the way they all did. No one ever opened it wide so the person could walk right in. They never knew whether it might be a tramp woman like Goody Good, with a half-snarled demand for food, saying she was freezing or starving, or an Indian. It might be a harmless Bible Indian, and then again, people had foolishly opened the door wide and found an Indian brave in full regalia—his face daubed with paint, his feathered headdress quivering, his nostrils flared, his eyes contemptuous—tomahawk in hand——

"Oh," Abigail said, and opened the door wide. " 'Tis Anne Putnam, Jr., and the Putnams' bound girl—Mercy. Come in quick, so the heat won't all be lost outside."

They took off their shawls and their heavy woolen

cloaks and their mittens. Anne warmed her hands before the fire. Mercy looked around the keeping room, eyeing the fire, the dark red curtains at the windows, the freshly sanded floor.

Mercy said, "I see you got a big fire going. Parson must have plenty of firewood." She put a basket down on the trestle table. "Mistress Putnam sent broth for Mistress Parris, and new baked bread, and hopes she'll soon be better." She looked at Tituba and then at Betsey who was sitting on Tituba's lap, Tituba's arms around her. "Is she sick, too?"

"No," Tituba said.

"Then why is a great girl like that lying in your lap? For shame!"

Tituba started to say Betsey is not a great girl—she is only six years old and quite small for her age. But Abigail spoke first. She said deliberately, carelessly, "She had some kind of fit. But she's all right now."

"A fit?" Mercy said, staring. "I didn't know Parson's daughter had fits. What kind of fit?"

"She seemed to go to sleep."

"Sleep aren't fits. With fits they fall down and froth at the mouth. Did she froth at the mouth?"

Abigail shook her head.

"That weren't a proper fit. With real fits they fall down. Sometimes they call it the falling sickness. Some places it's called the French king's sickness. Sometimes their tongues come way out of their mouths." Mercy's tongue protruded, demonstrating.

Tituba felt Betsey stiffen in her arms and knew she was frightened. She said, sharply, "You've the longest tongue

I've ever seen, miss. They do say liars have extra long tongues."

There was a hostile silence. Mercy turned her head away, took off her cap, ran her fingers through her yellow hair, said nothing.

Abigail said, "Tituba was telling us a story about Barbados—the island where she came from, where it's always warm. They don't have snow."

Anne Putnam, white-faced, as delicate-looking as Betsey, said very politely, "Tituba, tell us about the island. We can't stay very long. It gets dark early, and it's so cold outside." Then she added with a coaxing note in her voice, "If we heard about that warm place where you came from, it would help us keep warm on the way home. The thought of it would warm us."

"No," Tituba said firmly. "It is too late. You must get started now, or you will be going through the forest in the black dark."

She helped them with their shawls and their heavy cloaks, and made certain that they had put on their mittens before she opened the outer door. After they left she struggled to close the door. The air that came in felt like ice around her ankles. When she finally got it shut, she stood near the fire, warmed her hands, and then added another log, moved the black pot closer to the fire. Perhaps she should have told a story to Anne and Mercy. They had come two miles through the slush and snow; even jogging along on a farm horse it would be a cold trip going back.

The wind blew a sudden gust of smoke down the chimney. She drew back, eyes smarting, coughing. There was a knocking sound from upstairs. The mistress needed something.

"I'll go," Betsey said. "I'll go."

Betsey came back to report that the fire had gone out. Tituba and Abigail and Betsey carried wood upstairs, rebuilt the fire. Tituba got the mistress something hot to drink.

When the master came home he found them all upstairs. He was bursting with news. There was something triumphant about him, even the way he entered the room. He hadn't stopped to take off his greatcoat.

He bent over his wife, patted her hand. "Everything will be just as it should be." He straightened up, reached inside his coat, brought out a piece of paper.

"Listen," he said, "listen to this very carefully: 'January 2, 1690. To all Christian people to whom this present writing shall come, Nathaniel Ingersoll, of Salem Village, in the County of Essex, sendeth greeting. Know ye, that the said Nathaniel Ingersoll, husbandman, and Hannah, his wife, for and in consideration of the love, respect, and honor which they justly bear unto the public worship of the true and only God, and therefore for the encouragement of their well-beloved pastor, the Rev. Samuel Parris, who hath lately taken that office amongst them, and also for and in consideration of a very small sum of money to them in hand paid, with which they do acknowledge themselves fully contented and satisfied, do grant to said Samuel Parris and Elizabeth, his wife, for life, and then to the children of said Samuel and Elizabeth Parris, four and a half acres of land, adjoining upon the home field of the said Nathaniel Ingersoll; the three acres on the south alienated by gift, and the remainder by sale.' "

He let his breath out in a sigh. "We now have more land," he said. "There is a young orchard on it, and the trees bear fruit every year." He paced up and down the room. "With an orchard added to the ministry house and land, we'll be able to live like other folk—not always searching for a home provided by a congregation."

"This house isn't ours yet, is it, Samuel?" the mistress whispered.

"It is ours by agreement," he said sternly. "These are a stiff-necked people, but I will bend them. They will say it is ours, too—the Nurses, the Coreys, the Easteys, the Willards, the Hows, the Bradburys, the Porters, the Hutchinsons. I will bend all of those who now oppose me." In a quieter voice he said, "Let us join in a prayer of gratitude for this gift."

They knelt down by the bedframe in the mistress' room. The master was still wearing his greatcoat. Tituba opened her eyes and looked at him and thought, His face is wrathful, impatient even when he is praying.

Chapter 9

AFTER THE January thaw the days became perceptibly longer. By March there were signs of spring— bright green of skunk cabbage in the wet swampy places. The buds swelled on the maples and the ferns sent up brown fronds. In April, Tituba helped John plant corn. The farmers who stopped in at Ingersoll's told him how to plant it: fish heads in the bottom of the hills, four grains of corn to each hill—one for the blackbird, one for the crow, one for the farmer, and one to grow.

One man had said to him, whispering, hand held before his mouth to keep the sound from traveling, to keep anyone from reading his lips, "In the old country we didn't say, 'One for the farmer.' We always said, 'One for the corn goddess.' We said, 'One for the devil's bird, one for the crow, one for the corn goddess, and one to grow—' "

John said he'd whispered in reply, "Devil's bird?"

The man said, still whispering, still holding his hand in front of his mouth, "The yellow bird is the devil's bird. It doesn't eat the corn, just picks it out of the hill. Out of devilishness."

When Tituba worked in the garden, weeding on her

hands and knees or hoeing the weeds out of the corn, Puss, the money cat, accompanied her. He walked in and out under her skirt or poked delicately at her hand, pretending to pounce. He got entangled with the weeds, and sometimes loose dirt spattered over his varicolored fur, and then he would flatten his ears and his tail would switch in anger.

Now that spring had come, John was home every night. He stayed until midmorning, planting the minister's garden. Once again he brought them news of what went on all over the Colony. The men from Boston who came into the tavern were concerned about the new Massachusetts Charter, which would replace the one that had been revoked in 1684. Tituba was far more interested in what people were saying about the master. There was a gradual lessening in the quantity of provisions that was brought in to the ministry house.

John said the folk didn't say much about the master. Occasionally some said he was greedy, but they'd said that before. He had heard talk that the committee that had hired the master hadn't been told to promise him the ministry house. "Some say they don't want a minister who changed his mind about being a minister. He didn't finish his study at Harvard. He went into the West India trade instead. Then when he failed at that, why, he decided to be a minister and get himself property without working for it."

He leaned on his hoe and looked around at the cleared land. "It's a fair piece of land," he said. "They all know that it's good farm land—all cleared. A Mr. Burroughs got the stumps out. He was minister here once and a very strong man. They say only a thievish man would be so dead-set on owning a ministry house."

John built a fence of saplings to keep out deer and rabbits and woodchucks. He said it was called a palisade fence. One of the farmers gave them four young pigs, and he built a pen for pigs behind the barn. Tituba kept the pigs penned and fed them in the pen.

When John said, "Let them run free and root for themselves," she said, "I can't chase after pigs. This way I'll always know where they are."

By fall, John was building the minister another woodpile. Deacon Ingersoll sent Pim, the bound boy, to help him cut wood. John said Pim worked all right out in the woods. He was a strong boy, and if he had a mind to, he could work just like a man chopping wood.

Tituba felt more comfortable in her mind. They'd been all right so far. They would have plenty of food for the coming winter and plenty of wood. There were two cows in the barn and a mare and a big flock of chickens. The house was snug—the roof had been repaired and the chimneys cleaned out so they wouldn't catch on fire. The windows were clean. The paths had been weeded, and Tituba had defined their edges so they were clean-cut and straight, and had bordered them with flowers and herbs.

During the summer the mistress had been up and about, able to sew and to walk around outside. True, at the first hint of cold and dampness she had started to cough, and shortly after she had gone back to bed. But she looked better than she had ever looked while they were in Boston.

Sometimes in the morning, when Tituba went outside

to water the horse or feed the pigs, she stopped to stare into the stone watering trough. She had discovered that if she looked at it long enough, she could see things in it that were not there—not this pale blue sky, or the trees with their leaves beginning to turn red and gold and orange, or her own reflection. If she stared steadily with an unwinking gaze at the water in the trough, she imagined she saw the coral-encrusted coast line of Barbados, the palm trees, the dark green flags of the cane waving in the fields.

One morning she had a strange experience. She decided afterwards that she had had a genuine vision which permitted her to look straight into the future. When she stared into the watering trough she saw herself—dark brown dress, dark turban wrapped tightly around her head, a bit of white linen at her throat. She was standing alone on a table. People were seated around her, staring up at her, and their expressions were so angry that Tituba moved away from the trough, frightened.

She was so completely absorbed in her thoughts that she was unaware that Betsey had come out of the house and was standing quite close to her until Betsey tugged at her hand. "Titibee," she said, "what are you doing? Let me look, too. I want to see, too." She stared into the water in the trough. "What did you see just now when you looked in the water?"

"The island," she said, "and the blue water of the bay and the palm trees and the bright birds." And then she stopped and added truthfully, "and something I didn't understand. It frightened me to look at it."

Betsey, leaning over, staring, staring, said, "I can't see any of that. I see my own face. Very small, very small."

She pitched forward and would have fallen into the trough if Tituba hadn't caught her.

"You know, just that fast, I went to sleep. Looking at that water so long put me to sleep," Betsey explained.

Abigail, who had come out of the house to help carry water, heard Betsey's explanation and said, "You were having a fit. You weren't asleep."

"I was not. I don't have fits. Do I, Tituba? Do I?"

Tituba shook her head. "No," she said, "it's just that there are some people who can't look at water in a dish or at a round glass ball for a long time. It puts them to sleep."

Tituba hoped that Abigail would forget that Betsey had this strange ability to sleep or whatever it was that happened to her when she stared at something for too long a time. But Abigail did not forget.

It was almost a year later before Abigail deliberately induced a trancelike state in Betsey. During the months in between, they had survived another winter as severe as the previous one. Tituba had told many stories to the girls about Barbados and the guppy man who was so sly and so smart he could be in two places at once. John and Tituba had planted another garden and harvested the crop. Tituba had learned to reckon time the way the farmers did. She spoke of "sweet corn time" and "at the beginning of last hog time" or "in the middle of seed time for winter wheat." She learned this from John and Goodwife Mary Sibley. She knew when Goody Good had been in or around the barn by the smell that lingered in the air.

Puss, the money cat, was older and wiser. Abigail was

now eleven; Betsey was eight. The mistress spent less and less time in bed.

During those months, the relationship between the Reverend Samuel Parris and his parishioners had steadily worsened. Fewer and fewer of them attended the church meetings. On the Lord's Day many of them went to worship in the meetinghouse in the town of Salem ten miles away. They did not pay their rates to Reverend Parris— the money and provisions that represented their share of the cost of the support of the minister.

The meetinghouse roof leaked and was not repaired. Bats sometimes swooped down among the congregation.

In October, 1691, a town meeting elected a committee of five men to investigate all the circumstances involved in Mr. Parris settling among them and how Mr. Parris ever came to believe that he was to own the ministry house.

Tituba had never seen the master so angry. He paced up and down the floor of the keeping room most of the evening. He said the men named to the committee were his enemies. He named them: Joseph Porter, Joseph Hutchinson, Joseph Putnam, Daniel Andrew, Francis Nurse.

Every few days after that he called a church meeting. He held these meetings in the keeping room. Tituba sat in a shadowy corner beyond the reach of the firelight, listening to what was said. He told them that the committee appointed by the parish refused to set a rate for the minister. It was decided that the matter would have to be taken to court, the county court in Salem. Only five people came to that meeting.

This decision was reached on November 18, 1691. Tituba felt relieved. They could argue in the court in Salem, and she hoped that it would take weeks to decide the case so that the master's harsh voice and long prayers would be transferred to some other household. Thus these frequently held church meetings would come to an end.

That same day she discovered that Abigail had been placing bowls of water in front of Betsey, had been persuading her to stare into them. Tituba had started to enter the house from the lean-to in the back. She heard voices, and she paused, listening, one hand on the latch of the big wooden door that led into the keeping room. She recognized the voices as belonging to Abigail, Anne Putnam, Jr., and Mercy Lewis.

"Do you think she'll have one of her fits today?" Mercy Lewis asked.

Abigail's voice was light, higher in pitch. "I'll put a bowl of water on the table." Tituba could hear Abigail's quick footsteps, hear the sound of something being set down on the trestle table. "There," she said, "if she looks at it long enough she'll go journeying."

"How can she journey? Where does she go? She's right here in front of us. We can reach out and touch her. How can she go anywhere and still be here?" Anne Putnam's voice was a small hushed voice.

"Witches do," Mercy Lewis said. "A witch can be in bed and fast asleep, and her shape can be miles away, riding on a broomstick. I ride—I ride—I ride—" There was a galloping sound from inside.

"Hush!" Abigail said sharply. "Uncle Parris is in his study. He's working on his sermon. He can not abide noise. He will thrash all of us if we disturb him."

There was silence.

Anne Putnam said quietly, "Do you think Betsey will have a fit today? She didn't have one yesterday."

Abigail's voice was equally as quiet. "I don't know. I can't tell when she will and when she won't. She didn't have one yesterday because we were in the woods and she's scared of the woods. But if she looks at that bowl of water long enough— Hurry! She's coming downstairs. Everybody sit down at the table. Leave that place for Betsey—right there—in front of the bowl—"

Tituba gave them just enough time to get settled at the table, and then she entered the room.

"What errand brings you today?" she asked. She hung her shawl on a hook near the outer door.

"Mistress Putnam wondered if you could give her some of the iris tea you make for Mistress Parris. She has a griping in her side."

"Yes."

Betsey came into the room.

"Close the door," they shouted. "Close the door. Don't let the heat go up the stairs."

Betsey turned back and closed the door. Tituba sat down at the table in the place they had saved for Betsey. She glanced at the bowl of water, got up, removed it, saying, "I didn't know I'd left this on the table."

It was so quiet in the room that when a log fell forwards in the fire, sending up a shower of sparks, they all jumped.

Anne Putnam said, "Tituba, please tell us a story. We can't stay very long."

"No," she said. "I must be at the flax wheel. It's somebody else's turn. Mercy, you tell us a story."

Tituba sat down in front of the wheel, a little away from them. The whir of the wheel, the steady rhythmic thump of the pedal were the only sounds in the room. Puss jumped down from the settle and crouched at her feet. She pushed her long dark skirt over him, covering him up to tease him, and then wished that she hadn't. Mercy was watching her with a disapproving look that suggested she thought there was a suspicious intimacy between Tituba and the cat. She remembered what Goody Sibley had said about witches and the cats that were their familiars, "The devil gives them the cats to serve them and do their bidding."

Tituba said, "Tell us a story, Mercy."

"I can't tell stories," Mercy said sullenly. "I don't know any."

"Couldn't you tell us about Guppy, Tituba?" Betsey asked. "Just a little something? I like the Guppy stories."

Tituba pursed her lips, shook her head. "I can't talk and keep the thread thin and straight."

"Then we had all this walk for nothing and there's snow coming on and the wind is blowing and it's so cold out it is like being outdoors when you are bare naked." Mercy drew a deep breath. "They ought to put Tituba in the press yard," she said spitefully. "That would make her talk."

"What's the press yard?" Abigail asked.

"It's where they press the prisoners to death in the great prison in London. They roll stones on them until they die—bigger and bigger stones, heavier and heavier, until they press their insides right out. They press the ones who stand mute. They're the ones who won't answer questions. They won't say they're guilty, and they won't say they're not guilty."

Abigail said, "How do you know about it?"

"Pim, the bound boy at Ingersoll's, told me. He says the smell in the press yard is something dreadful."

They stared at her in dismay. Betsey burst into tears.

Anne said, "A place like that must be filled with ghosts." Then she covered her face with her hands and said, her voice muffled, "I shall dream about it all night."

The money cat left the shelter of Tituba's long dark skirt and scratched at the outside door.

"It's cold out there," Tituba said. "Are you sure you want to go out?"

The cat mewed as though in answer. Tituba got up, opened the door, and the cat went out quickly, tail up in the air, ears slightly flattened against his skull. As she closed the door behind him, she heard Mercy's shocked whisper, "Ooo-ooo-h! The cat answered her. Did you hear him?"

Tituba pretended she hadn't heard this. She stood in front of the fire, warming herself. The room had cooled off quickly. Betsey had her head down on the table, still weeping. The others shivered because of the cold air that had come into the room. She found herself feeling sorry for them. They would spend most of the winter indoors. They would have chills and fevers; they would cough and blow their noses from now until spring came. On the Lord's Day they would sit hunched over in the meetinghouse, listening to the master's long sermons and his long prayers.

"I'll tell you a very short story about how the monkey picked out a wife for Guppy," she said as she sat down at the table. "Monkey went to a simpler—"

"What's a simpler?" Anne Putnam asked.

"You're not to ask any questions when I'm telling the story," she said severely. "Next time I won't go on." She was silent for so long that the girls shifted uneasily.

She said, "The simpler gave Monkey a piece of dried root—very dark in color and very shriveled. He told him how to boil it and then add a little vinegar to it and then boil it some more and see that Mr. Guppy drank it. Mr. Guppy would go to sleep, and then Monkey must talk to Mr. Guppy, telling him what he was to do the next day. Mr. Guppy would have a dream, and the next day Mr. Guppy would do just what he'd done in the dream.

"So Monkey did what the simpler told him to do. He forgot that Mr. Guppy was a man and not a monkey. Monkey got quite carried away with talking about courtship and marriage. He described the lady monkey that he wanted to marry, and he sang the song that he had made in honor of the lady monkey.

"Early the next morning, Mr. Guppy got up, put on his finest suit of clothes, and went to the edge of the jungle and called out and then sang. Very soon a delicately built, very beautiful little lady monkey leaned out from the branch of a tree, swung by her tail in time to the music of the song, and then jumped down on Mr. Guppy's shoulder. She sat there, her tail hanging down his back, one of her small cold paws grasping his ear. Mr. Guppy was delighted. He took her back home with him, and he still has her there. He sings Monkey's song to her every day, and sometimes he walks into the village carrying her on his shoulder. He can not understand why Monkey sits in a tree and screams when he goes past."

Tituba stood up. "It's time for you to go home."

"Is that all there is?" Mercy asked. When Tituba nodded, she said, "When we come again, will you tell us some more?"

Before Tituba could answer, Anne Putnam said, "What's a simpler?"

"It's a man or a woman who gathers herbs and sells them. Herbs are called simples. The person who gathers and sells them is known as a simpler. People go to them to get cures for diseases."

They were slow to leave. Tituba urged them gently towards the door, saying, "Is this your shawl, Mercy?"

"What's a jungle?" Anne Putnam asked.

"It is like your great forest—not easy to walk through. Filled with birds. Sometimes there are monkeys. It is warm and moist, and steam rises from the ground."

"Is it always warm in a jungle?" Mercy asked.

"Indeed, yes."

"There is no winter?"

"No. People do not have to wear heavy cloaks and shawls." She took Anne Putnam's cloak from a hook near the door. "Here's your cloak."

Instead of putting the cloak on, Anne Putnam said, "What do monkeys look like, Tituba?"

"Well—" she said, frowning and at a loss for words with which to describe a monkey. "Well—he is a small beast with short hair and paws that he uses like folk use their hands. He makes a chattering noise."

"Do monkeys have the power of speech?" Anne Putnam asked.

"Only in the stories that folk make up about them."

"Could you sing us his song—the one the monkey sang in your story?"

Tituba opened the door wide, and freezing cold air rushed into the room. "No," she said. "I couldn't. Now hurry along before the whole house is cold."

Chapter 10

TITUBA simply could not keep track of the girls any more. If she went into the barn, she heard snatches of whispered conversation from a shadowy corner, "Let me ask her a question," or "Look at the water, Betsey. Keep looking at the water, Betsey." They were always together—Anne Putnam, Jr., Mercy Lewis, Mary Walcott, Abigail—in the dooryard, behind the barn, in the keeping room.

She scolded; she threatened them. They pretended they did not know what she was talking about. They smiled at her; their faces and eyes were innocent, without guile.

Abigail would shrug and say, "Sometimes she has fits, Tituba. You know that. We don't do anything—"

Betsey cried easily. Any sudden movement, any loud sound affected her. Even the unexpected sight of her own shadow on the wall would make her jump and say, "What's that?"

Another time, Tituba had been upstairs. When she came down, the keeping room seemed full of girls. Anne Putnam, Jr., Mercy Lewis, Abigail Williams, Betsey Parris, and Elizabeth Hubbard were sitting at the trestle table. Mary Walcott was seated on a settle near the fire.

Betsey's eyes were open, but she was staring straight ahead of her, her gaze fixed and unwinking. Mercy Lewis was bending over her saying, "Did the Reverend George Burroughs kill you?"

Betsey spoke in a low, guttural voice. Her breathing was labored and slow. "Yes, he killed his first two wives, and he killed me." She paused and added, "There's more to tell—"

Mercy said, "What did you say?"

Tituba took hold of Betsey's wrist and pressed gently, firmly, "Betsey," she said, "Betsey, it's time to wake up."

The child shuddered, blinked her eyes and moaned, "Oh, Titibee—Titibee—"

Tituba scowled at the girls. They looked ashamed and afraid, heads hung down. Only Abigail looked back at her.

"I've told you again and again not to do this. You'll harm the child—" There was a bright, shiny sixpence in the bowl of water.

"We only did it for sport," Mercy Lewis said.

She looked more frightened than the others. After all, she was a bound girl. Tituba thought, I will get her in trouble if I tell on her. She knows this. Anne Putnam is a deacon's daughter and Mary Walcott is the Sibleys' niece —they're big landowners, and they contribute heavily to the church, so no one will do anything to Mary Walcott. But Mercy Lewis? She was lively, rosy-cheeked. She had bright yellow hair that was always tumbling down from under her cap. The people would say she was dabbling in the black arts, that she was trying to talk to the dead. They'd put her in the stocks, have her whipped at the whipping post—they might hang her.

Tituba said, "I told you—" She frowned. While her attention was centered on Betsey, one of them had taken the six-pence out of the bowl of water. They were all looking at her with blank faces. It would be impossible to say who had removed the coin—their hands were folded in their laps. But she knew one of them must have a wet hand. And as though they'd read her thoughts, they leaned over the table and began playing in the water, dabbling their fingers in it. Now they all had wet hands; they dried them on their long skirts, smiling faintly.

Mercy Lewis reached inside the bodice of her long gown. She had a package tucked inside. She put it down on the table and unwrapped it. Tituba watched her, wondering what it was that was so precious that she carried it tucked inside her bodice.

It was a pack of playing cards. Mercy spread them out on the trestle table. "They're playing cards. I got them from Pim, the redheaded boy at Deacon Ingersoll's."

Anne Putnam frowned. "We can't have those here. It's sinful."

"No more sinful than your talk of ghosts and wanting to talk to the dead," Abigail said. "I've never seen playing cards before. Let me hold them, Mercy. They're pretty, aren't they? There are so many of them."

Betsey said, "I don't think we should have playing cards here in the ministry house. There's so much talk against Father in the Village—if it were known—"

"What kind of talk is there against him?" Abigail kept

picking the cards up and looking at them. Tituba knew that she only asked this question to distract Betsey's attention.

"The people say we have no right to this house. They say unkind things about us." Betsey put her hand on Abigail's arm and said, "I don't think we should have these cards here."

Abigail said, "They're just heavy paper and they have pictures on them. Pictures of people. Kings and queens. They're such pretty colors." She spread them out even farther. "I wish I had these for my own. Think of all the games I could play with them. I could match the pictures and—"

Tituba picked up some of the cards. It was a very pretty deck, very skillfully painted. The edges were gilded. She thought, Why this is a fortune-telling deck—a tarot deck. It's not for games and gambling. She used to tell Mistress Endicott's fortune with cards like these.

"Where'd a bound boy get cards like these?" she asked.

"A gentleman gave them to him," Mercy said. She looked rather pleased to be the center of attention. "A very great lord gave them to him before he left London. 'Pim,' he said, 'these are my favorite cards. I'm giving them to you as a farewell present.'"

"And Pim gave them to you?"

Mercy flushed. "Well—no—he loaned them to me. He said—well, he said, maybe I could find someone to teach me how to tell fortunes. Then I could tell his fortune."

There was a silence in the room, a strange perturbed silence. They all looked at Tituba.

Abigail said, "Is that what these cards are for?" She

looked at Tituba, her mouth slightly open. "Tituba, you can tell fortunes. You told me you could. Tell my fortune, please, Tituba. Here." She pushed the cards toward Tituba.

Tituba hesitated. All of her instincts told her not to do this. But what harm can it do? she thought. She sat down at the table, picked up part of the deck, and shuffled the cards so expertly they must have known she had done this many times before. It was like being in Barbados, sitting across the table from Mistress Endicott. Except that this table was pine and light in color, and the table they'd used in Barbados was polished mahogany and it had gleamed in the candlelight.

"Pick a card," she said to Abigail. "Now pick another card." She began lining the cards up on the table.

Someone knocked at the outside door. With a deft movement Tituba swept the cards together, handed them to Mercy Lewis. She did not wait to see where Mercy put the cards. She walked slowly to the door, opened it only a crack.

Mary Warren, the bound girl at the Proctors', stood at the door. She had a big haunch of meat in her arms, and Tituba thought, More fodder for the minister. Mary Warren had dark, slightly protruding eyes, and she kept trying to see into the room.

"My master, John Proctor, sent meat for the minister. Please to see that it's put in the rate book." She said this quickly as though she had memorized it, even imitating the intonation of her master's voice. But she couldn't copy the texture of his voice. Tituba remembered his voice as being pleasant to the ear. This girl's voice was coarse and unpleasant.

I'll have to let her in, Tituba thought. She's come all the way from the Proctors' farm. She looks frozen, nose red and pinched, cheeks roughened and reddened from the cold, teeth chattering. Another of these bound girls. But this one was older than the others. She was closer to twenty. John Proctor was said to be a hard taskmaster despite his pleasant-sounding voice. He had a reputation for thrashing the girls who worked there. He wanted them to spin and weave and fetch and carry, without respite. Surely before the girl turned around and went back, surely she should be allowed to warm herself by the fire.

"Come inside," Tituba said.

The girl looked surprised when she saw Mercy Lewis and Anne Putnam, Jr., and Elizabeth Hubbard and Mary Walcott sitting at the table with Abigail and Betsey. She greeted them, but she kept staring at them, and finally she said, "What are you doing?"

They all smiled at once—false, forced smiles. Tituba thought anyone could tell their smiles weren't genuine. They were making themselves smile, and they were half-frightened.

Abigail, the quick-witted, quick-speeched one, said, "We were telling stories."

"Oh." Mary Warren pulled off her mittens, hung her cloak on a hook by the door. "I—could I listen?"

"You're too late. We just finished and they're getting ready to go home." Abigail looked hard at Mercy Lewis.

Mercy stood up, and so did the others. As Mercy walked toward the door, a card dropped on the floor, and then another, and then another. She was leaving a little trail of fortune-telling cards behind her as she walked.

Tituba watched in dismay. They all did.

Mary Warren pointed. "What are those? What has she got there?" And then squealing, "Look what's coming out of her!"

"A friend—" Mercy stammered. "I had to keep them for a friend. The boy at the—"

Abigail interrupted. "A bound boy found them, and his master saw them, and he had to pretend he didn't have them, that he'd burned them up. Mercy's keeping them for him."

"What are they?"

"Pictures," Abigail said. "Pictures of kings and of queens and court jesters and farmers and soldiers." She started picking up the cards. "And a man that was hanged —just pictures. Very pretty pictures. Like little paintings."

Mary Warren helped pick up the cards. She placed them on the table. "Can I keep one? This pretty one of a king? I'd put it somewhere safe and take it out and look at it sometimes. I'd never tell I got it in the minister's house."

Abigail gathered all the cards together. "No," she said. "She's keeping them for a bound boy. She can't give any away."

Abigail put them in a neat pile and then patted the top card. Without thinking, Tituba sorted them out, counted them, handed them to Mercy.

"They're all there."

"How do you know?" Mary Warren asked. "How do you know how many there should be?"

Abigail said quickly, "We counted them when Mercy showed them to us."

"Who counted them?"

"Tituba."

"Can you count up that high?" Mary Warren eyed the stack of cards. "How'd you learn to count?"

"In Barbados. A long time ago." John had taught her to count, slowly, laboriously. She practiced and practiced. When he got a big catch, she counted fish; she counted eggs in the market; she counted Mistress Endicott's shoes and her petticoats—she had owned twenty-five petticoats. John had taught her to make figures, too.

The cards were still on the table. Mercy had her hand lifted to pick them up when Betsey said, "Tituba, tell Mercy not to bring those fortune-telling cards here again."

"Fortune-telling cards!" Mary Warren said, aghast.

Abigail reached across the table and slapped Betsey's face, slapped her so hard that the blow left a red mark on the soft white skin. Betsey screamed and started to cry.

"You fool, you tattletale. You've spoiled everything. You always do—"

Mercy Lewis said, "Hit her again, Abigail. Hit her again."

Mary Walcott said, "Good for you, Abigail."

Abigail lifted her hand towards Betsey, and Tituba pulled her away. She shook Abigail, saying, "Don't do that again."

Mary Warren put her hands on her hips and laughed and laughed and laughed. The raucous sound she made seemed to echo in the room, to run along under the beams, to linger and reverberate through the bundles of dried herbs hanging from the soot-darkened rafters.

"It's like a show," she said. "I wouldn't have missed it for anything. She"—pointing at Mercy Lewis—"gets up to go home and cards fall out of her clothes, just like she was sowing seed. But it's cards instead. This one"—pointing at Abigail Williams— "says they're pictures, pretty little pictures of kings and queens. Like paintings."

She stopped laughing, and there was a gloating sound in her voice. "They're cards to tell fortunes with. And they're right here in the minister's house. Wait till I tell Master. Wait till Master Proctor hears that Deacon Putnam's daughter was here, and the minister's daughter and the minister's niece were here."

She started laughing again. "Ha, ha, ha! They'll switch you, and they'll put you in the stocks, and the bound boys will throw mud and filth on you. Ha, ha, ha!"

Betsey cried out in fear. Abigail pinched her on the arm, twisting the soft flesh between her fingers.

Tituba pinched Abigail's arm the same way, only her fingers were stronger than Abigail's and so it was a much more painful pinch. Abigail shrieked, "I hate you," and started to cry, too.

Mary Warren said, "Ooo-hh, I can't wait to get home. Ooo-hh. I can't wait." She hurried towards the door, one work-worn hand reaching out to open it, and she began to laugh again.

Abigail took a deep breath, choked back her sobs, and followed Mary to the door. She said, "Wouldn't you like to have your fortune told?"

Mary Warren didn't bother to turn around. She shook her head, put her cloak around her shoulders.

Abigail moved closer. "Wouldn't you like to know who you're going to marry? And if you're going to have a farm or live in a fine house in Boston? Wouldn't you like to know if you'll have servants so you can box their ears and beat them with brooms? Wouldn't you like to find out?"

"Find out how?"

"It's all in the cards. Tituba can tell you. She can read the cards."

"Has she read yours?"

"No."

"How do you know she can do it?"

"Ask her."

"Can you?" Mary said, the cloak still half around her but the work-worn hands no longer clutching at it in haste.

Tituba thought, If I tell her fortune then she won't tell about these cards being in the master's house. But this is not good. These girls keep adding to the things that go on here that can't be talked about. This will cause trouble for all of us.

Abigail said, "She learned from her old mistress in Barbados. Come, Tituba, sit here at the table and tell Mary Warren what's in the cards for her. Give me the cards, Mercy."

Mercy said, "I've got to go."

"If you don't give me those cards, I'll tell on you. I'll tell what you keep asking Betsey."

Mercy laid the cards down on the table. They all sat

down. Tituba shuffled the cards. They slipped softly against each other. She spread the pack face up on the table, placing the cards in rows.

"Now," she said to Mary Warren. "Look at the cards, think about the cards. No one must speak."

Tituba kept them waiting so long that when she finally spoke, breaking the silence, she heard them exhale and knew they had been sitting there, tense, hardly daring to breathe. She said that Mary Warren was going to marry a rich Boston merchant, that she would live in a fine big house and have many servants.

Then she stopped talking, troubled because the cards did not say this. The cards said people would hang because of Mary Warren. Tituba felt ashamed to be falsifying the message of the cards. But unless Mary Warren left the minister's house excited and happy by the thought of what the future held for her, she would surely tell her master that there were fortune-telling cards in use in the home of the pious Mr. Parris.

Tituba shuffled the cards again and laid them out on the table. She could tell that this was a new deck by the smooth slick feel of the cards.

She made no mention of hangings. She said, "You will lose something of value on the way home."

"Ah," Mary Warren said. "What will I lose? What is it?"

Tituba didn't answer.

Abigail said, "You've broken the spell, you stupid thing. She told you not to talk. She can't see any more now."

"She can't see what?"

"She can't see the meaning. She and Betsey can some-times tell what's going to happen. They see it. They see the meaning of things."

Mary Warren looked at Tituba in open-mouthed amazement. Tituba picked up the cards, stacked them in a neat pile, handed it towards Mercy Lewis.

Abigail plucked the cards out of Tituba's hand. "I'll keep them in a safe place," she said.

"I've got to give them back," Mercy protested.

"Not yet. I'll keep them for you."

Mary Warren said, "You said I'd marry a rich mer-chant. A rich Boston merchant."

Her face was transformed, the expression softened, yearning. She wouldn't live on a farm any more, wouldn't freeze in the winter, wouldn't be boxed on the ear and screamed at by a lazy, scolding mistress, whipped by an impatient master. She would think about her good fortune all the way home—plenty of candles, fine clothes from London, a house filled with silver and fine furniture.

She paused at the door, remembering. "Tituba, what will I lose? What will I lose on the way home?"

Tituba shook her head. "I don't know. Next time, don't talk."

As she closed the door behind Mary Warren, she thought, there will be no next time. But she was wrong.

Chapter 11

THE NEXT morning Tituba was halfway up the steep stairs with an armload of wood when someone banged at the back door. She hurried up the stairs, put the wood in the woodbox in the mistress' room. She glanced around the low-ceilinged bedroom. The mistress looked quite bright, shawl around her shoulders. She was sitting up in the middle of the bed, eating porridge. Abigail and Betsey were sitting on the edge of the bed, talking to her. Pale morning sunlight came through the two front windows.

There was another banging at the door. Tituba said, "I'll bring you cider when I come back."

Just as she reached the keeping room, the master came out of his study. "I'll go to the door. I didn't know you were upstairs. It's probably Deacon Ingersoll."

He opened the door wide, and then he drew back. Tituba recognized the smell and the ragged clothing. It was Goody Good. She walked right past the master into the keeping room. She said no word of greeting. She had a very small child by the hand.

The master backed away from her. A rush of cold air and a terribly sour smell pervaded the room. The master closed the door.

Abigail and Betsey came downstairs, saw Goody Good, and stood close together, watching her. From somewhere inside the rags she pulled out a pipe, leaned over the fire, and, seizing a thin shaving, set it ablaze and lit the pipe. She puffed a cloud of rank-smelling smoke in the master's face and set him to coughing.

"We've come beggin'," she said. "We need food, Minister."

The child peered out at them, holding tight to its mother's ragged dirty skirts, hardly daring to show all of its face, as though it thought harm could come to it from the direct glances of other people. It was snuffling like all these children in this cold damp climate. Tituba couldn't remember whether it was a girl or a boy. Then she recalled the child's name—Dorcas. A girl, of course.

"You're Sarah Good, aren't you?" the master said, frowning.

"If I must tell, I must tell. Yes, I am Goodwife Good."

The master shook his head. "The folk complain of you. They say you set fire to their barns with your pipe. They say you carry the smallpox. They say you steal—chickens and turkeys. They—"

"They lie. They lie," she said fiercely. "Who says this?" she peered at him, eyes gleaming under the matted gray hair. "We need food, Minister. 'Do unto others as ye would have them do unto you.' We need food. Dorcas and I are hungered."

"Give her whatever you can spare, Tituba."

"Little enough that'll be, Minister. Little enough I'm sure."

Tituba watched him, thinking, He moves away from the smell of her and the look of her. She's like a wild animal. She has a liar's gap in the front of her teeth. Or perhaps it's just that her teeth are missing and there's a space in the front. The rest of her teeth are black. Her hair is matted, and the smell of her chokes me.

Abigail said, "You don't have any manners, do you? You should be grateful."

Tituba thought, Why did she say that? There's no need to anger the creature. Best feed her in silence and let her go quickly.

"I should be grateful, eh, miss? Well, I'm not. Minister's fodder don't cost him. I haven't et for two days. Neither has this little child." She thrust the child forward, "Dorcas, you sit down."

"Sit at the table," Tituba said. She put portions of stewed rabbit on trenchers, poured cider into mugs, and gave them each a big piece of johnnycake. They drank the cider noisily, making sucking noises. They smacked their lips as they ate, blew on the hot meat as though they were horses noisily exhaling their breath. The child made a humming sound and rocked back and forth as it ate.

The master left the keeping room and quietly closed the door of his study. Betsey had taken refuge on a settle, a good distance away from them, and sat watching them with a little frown between her eyes. Abigail, who could never mind her own affairs, sat down at the table across from them, watching them eat, staring at them.

Faintly from upstairs came the rap on the floor that

meant the mistress needed something. Tituba told Abigail to find out what her Aunt Parris wanted.

Abigail scrambled up from the table hurriedly, impatience in each jerky movement. Good stared at her, black eyes slightly protruding, the expression malicious.

Tituba was pouring out more cider, and she stopped, pitcher lifted, forgetting what she was doing. For as Abigail stamped towards the door that led to the stairs—expressing her distaste for this command that would remove her from the keeping room, remove her for even a moment from the sight of these hungry tramps, shoulders jerking, switching her hips—the bound boy's fortune-telling cards started to fall. She was doing exactly what Mercy Lewis had done; she was leaving a trail of cards behind her. Some of them lay on the floor face up; some of them face down. Tituba was certain that this dirty tramp of a woman with the protruding eyes, with the sharp tongue of a scold, would never believe that they were pretty pictures that the minister's niece had had concealed about her person.

Even her reaction was indicative of the kind of problem she would pose. She laughed. It was a cackle, high in pitch, like the laughter of a crone, of a witch. Tituba thought, Why did I think that? Why that word? Because she looks the way John said the Witch Glover looked when she was hanged in Boston. Black eyes, malicious expression, matted hair.

Abigail turned when she heard Good laughing. She saw the cards on the floor, and her face reddened. She started to say something and stopped.

Good got up from the table, poked at the cards with a

dirty finger, turned them over. "They be fortune-telling cards. Tee-hee-hee. And in the minister's house. What be ye doing with a tarot pack, miss?"

Abigail, usually quick-witted, quick-talking, said nothing. She picked up the cards. Tituba helped her, thinking, If she hadn't been trying to let me know how cross she was by the way she walked, those cards would have stayed where she put them. Abigail put all the cards together in a pile on the table.

Good said peremptorily, "Answer me. What be ye doing with these cards?"

"They're not mine. I was keeping them for a friend."

Good laughed again. "I'll tell Minister. And, ah, but ye'll be whipped, miss. I'll stay and watch. Minister!" she said in a loud voice.

The door of the study is a thick one. She'll have to knock on his door or call louder, really shout, Tituba thought. To her surprise, Abigail, who couldn't abide messes, couldn't empty slops, couldn't stir the soap because the horrid mess might get on her hands, couldn't pull weeds out of onions because her hands would get dirty, put her hand firmly across Good's dirt-embedded face, covering her mouth, pressing the frowzy head with its matted hair against her own chest.

"No," she whispered. "No! What do you want? What'll you take? I have a little gold chain. I'll give it to you, but you mustn't tell—I won't let you tell—"

Good pushed her away with a sudden violent thrust of arms and body. Abigail fell down with a thud. Tituba thought, This will bring the master out of his study. The sound of a body hitting the floor was unmistakable—nothing else sounded like that.

The master opened his study door, looked into the room. "What was that?" he asked.

Abigail got up hastily. "I fell over the cat."

"It must have been a turn of the ankle. A twist of the heel," Good said. "Because the cat is outside. More cider, Tituba," she said agreeably. "And more of the rabbit. Did ye catch the rabbit, Minister, or is this some of the fodder that the farmers pitchfork into ye house?"

The master said, "Are you hurt, Abigail?"

"No, Uncle Parris. I must have—fallen over something. I don't know what. I'm not hurt."

Tituba thought, How quickly everything has changed. The cards are gone. Good must have snatched them up. Abigail doesn't look frightened—her cheeks are rosy; her eyes are bright. But her breathing is just a little faster than usual.

Dorcas, Good's child, had ignored everything and gone on eating hungrily and noisily, bent over the trencher as though she were a little pig at a trough. She took a drink of cider, and Tituba thought her hand was so thin and bony it was more like a bird's claw than the hand of a human being. She supposed the child was so accustomed to the trouble that took place everywhere they went that she paid no attention to it but tried to eat as much as she could before they were told to leave.

The master frowned at Good, nodded to Tituba. She refilled Good's trencher with rabbit, poured more cider into the mugs, divided the last of the johnnycake between them. The child's dirty little hand clutched at the johnny-cake.

The master had barely closed the door of his study behind him when Abigail said, "Give me my cards!"

"Thought you said they was a friend's cards."

"What difference does it make? Give them back."

Good began eating faster and faster. "Fetch your gold chain." Abigail hesitated. "Fetch it, I said, or I'll tell the minister. I'll tell the minister about ye having them dreadful cards. I'll throw them all over the floor again and tell him they fell out of your clothes, miss. And he'll have to leave here. When I tell the folk what I seen right here in the ministry house, they'll run him out of the Village."

Abigail got the gold chain quickly. It was as though she'd flown up and down the stairs. She said, "You won't get the chain until you give me the cards," dangling a thin golden chain in front of Good.

Betsey said, "Oh, isn't it beautiful?"

Good's eyes followed the movement of the chain. She reached out for it, and Abigail moved it away from her. "I'll have both," she said. "I'll have me the gold chain and the cards, too. Or I'll tell—I'll tell—"

Tituba intervened. "I'll not let you come in here and upset us with your threats. Go ahead," she said. "Throw the cards on the floor and call the master. I'll say the cards are mine."

"Ye think that sounds any better? The cards belong to the minister's black slave? Ye think they'd let him stay in the Village with a fortune-telling slave? Ye think they'd believe he didn't know that's what ye did? Oh, I hear 'em. I hear 'em. The farmers say he wants what isn't his. They say he's got a greed for land—"

She stopped talking and laughed, "Tee-hee. Tee-hee. Minister!" she shouted, and banged on the table with her mug, "Minister!" her voice carrying, rising in pitch.

The master appeared in the door, frowning, "Did someone call?" he asked.

"No," Abigail said. "No. Goodwife Good was telling how when Mr. Burroughs was the minister, Goody Osburne would call him to come to see her first husband. The one that died. Mr. Prince was her first husband, and he sickened and died, and Goody Osburne would stand outside this house and call, 'Minister! Minister!' " Abigail's voice was an exact imitation of Good's. "That was all. Nobody called you."

Dorcas went on eating noisily. Good leered at Abigail. There was a thump at the door.

Tituba opened it, and the money cat came in, lifting his feet high, his tail straight up in the air. He rubbed against Tituba's skirt, purring. Then he stood still and sniffed the air, and his tail swelled in size, and he hissed and ran towards the door. Tituba let him out, thinking, I don't blame him, no clean-living cat would stay in the room with the terrible smell of this woman.

"I said ye didn't fall over the cat, didn't I? Didn't I? And it's a money cat, a good-luck cat. Must be Tituba's cat. She would have a money cat—"

"Yes," Abigail said quietly. She was quite pale. "Yes to everything you said"—then quickly, talking faster and faster—"You say everything twice, so, yes, you said I didn't fall over the cat. That's what you said. That's what you said. So yes to everything."

The master said, "Stop this chattering," and went back in his study and closed the door.

Abigail sighed. She dropped the little gold chain into Good's outstretched hand.

"That's a pretty thing," Good said, holding it up in front of her, turning it, dangling it. "Ye'll be safe for quite a while, miss." The chain disappeared somewhere in the flutter of rags that was her skirt. She fumbled through her rags and produced the cards. She put them on the table.

"I want my fortune told," she said boldly. "Can ye read 'em?"

Abigail shook her head.

To Tituba's surprise, Betsey, who never interfered, who always stayed silent, said, "Tituba can tell your fortune. She learned how in Barbados."

"Tell my fortune," Good ordered.

Tituba said, "The minister's black slave doesn't tell fortunes for tramps. You have the child's golden chain and the child's cards. That's enough. Be off."

"If I give her back the chain will ye tell my fortune?"

Betsey said, "Oh, Tituba, please do. The gold chain belonged to Abigail's mother. If you'll tell Good's fortune, Abigail will get the chain back. It's such a little thing for you to do."

Abigail said plaintively, "It's the only thing I have that belonged to my mother."

"I'll not do it now. You come back when the master is not here, and you give the child her chain, and then I'll tell your fortune." Tituba held up her hands, checking the items off on her fingers. "First, the master will not be home. Second, you will give Abigail her gold chain. And then I will see what's in the cards for you."

Though it was very cold outside, they aired out the keeping room after Good and her child left. She kept looking back at them as she went out the door, her gaze malevolent, and she muttered to herself, "I'll be back. I'll be back." They let the door stay open. The money cat came in, sniffed the air, and left again, ears flattened against his skull. The keeping room grew colder and colder. Tituba sent the little girls upstairs where it was warmer.

Tituba washed the table, washed the bench, washed the floor, scoured it and sanded it. She could still smell Goody Good. She put a cedar log on the fire, scattered a little grated nutmeg on it. There was a faint fragrance in the room, and gradually it overcame the sour smell of Good. She closed the outside door, thinking, Not good to burn cedar too often, not good for the eyes, and set to work to prepare the food for their noonday meal. It was surprising how much Goody Good and Dorcas had eaten.

When Abigail and Betsey came downstairs, Abigail frowned, wrinkling her nose. The kitchen had warmed up. It smelled of cedar wood and of spices. Something delicious smelling was bubbling in the big iron pot, and the cedar logs were burning with a hot, brilliant, flaring flame.

"This room smells good," she said. "But I don't. I can still smell that horrible old witch where her head leaned against my dress."

"Why do you call her a witch?" Betsey asked.

"Because she put a spell on me. She made me drop those cards. Now she's got my gold chain, and she's got the cards, too." To Tituba's surprise, Abigail burst into tears.

Chapter 12

MERCY LEWIS was running pell-mell through the woods. She kept looking over her shoulder. She was alone and frightened. She had finally managed to slip out of the house without Anne Putnam. She was going to the minister's house to get the fortune-telling cards. She had to give them back to Pim.

The last time she went to Deacon Ingersoll's, sent on an errand by Mistress Putnam, Pim had cornered her in the outer hall, whispered fiercely, "Give me back my cards!"

She had made her voice low and soft, "I haven't got them," she said, smiling at him, thinking to beguile him, trying to move away from him. He kept following her until he had her backed against the wall, and he put his hands on the wall on each side of her so that she was caged there.

"Where are they?"

His breath was in her face, and he smelt of onions, and she turned her head away. "At the minister's."

He grabbed one of her hands and held it and bent it back. His hands felt like iron hoops. He kept bending her hand and her wrist, back and back. She didn't scream for fear someone would come out of the taproom, and he'd say, "My cards are at the minister's house. Mercy Lewis, the Putnams' bound girl, took them there." Not even playing cards, but real fortune-telling cards.

"Ah, don't," she gasped. "Don't—"

"Stop lying then. Where are my cards?"

His face had crimsoned, and with the bright carrot-colored hair above the red face, he looked like a demon. She thought her wrist was going to snap in two, and he looked so furious and so dangerous that she closed her eyes. He'd probably sold his soul to the devil long ago, and it wasn't even safe to look at him.

The hall door opened, and Goody Ingersoll said, "Pim!"

He dropped Mercy's wrists and turned away from her faster than she'd ever seen anyone move.

Goody Ingersoll said, "You look all fussed up. What's the matter with you?"

Pim said, "I've been hurrying," and went into the taproom and grabbed a birch broom and started sweeping the hearth, raising clouds of dust.

"Don't loiter there in the hall, girl. Come in or else go out. All you lazy thriftless girls hang around the bound boys. Come, come. Maybe a box on the ear will speed you."

Mercy delivered the message to Goody Ingersoll and hurried back home. Her wrist still ached. She hadn't dared go near Ingersoll's since then.

She was just beginning to be friendly with Pim when he had loaned her those cards. He said he didn't know how to tell fortunes and he ached to know what was in the cards for him. She'd said, I'll find someone who can teach me, and then I'll be able to tell your fortune, and mine, too.

They were beautiful cards, brightly colored, and the edges were shiny as though they were gilded. Abigail had taken them away from her. Abigail was like a cat—sly and quick and thievish. Well, she thought, you might as well say she was thievish. She stole the cards. If you take someone else's belongings without asking them, it was stealing.

She had to stop running to catch her breath. When she started off again, she told herself to walk slowly. But every sound made her hurry along faster and faster. Sometimes a great branch fell out of a tree, making a crashing sound, enough to scare a body out of their wits. There were rustling noises overhead, but she couldn't see what caused them. She caught glimpses of the cotton tails of rabbits. Squirrels and chipmunks ran up and down the trunks of trees.

As she approached Deacon Ingersoll's she left the trodden path and went deeper into the woods, keeping out of sight, ducking behind trees, and staying there when she heard the jingle of harness. Once when she peered out cautiously it was a farmer jogging along on a nag. Another time it was the Reverend Samuel Parris on Ingersoll's fine brown mare. Nobody knew why Ingersoll should have given that mare to the minister.

When she went on her way again, she kept looking up because of a sudden movement overhead in the branches of a tree, and then looking down because she thought something moved in the thickly piled leaves along the path. She climbed over fallen trees, skirting thickets of brambles, avoiding wet sedgy places. She kept making small sounds of fear under her breath, "Oh! Oh! What was that? Oh! Oh!" Once she fell flat on her face, and she was so tired and so frightened that she simply lay there, listening to a terrible thumping noise, shocked when she realized she was making it herself, the sound of her own heartbeats.

When she got up, she felt rested. She thought, I'm bigger than Abigail, and I'm older than she is, and I'll catch her out behind the minister's barn and take the cards away from her. Once I've got them, I'm going to throw them in the bound boy's face.

She heard the jingle of harness again and ducked behind a tree and peered around it to see who it was. Anne Putnam, Jr., went past on Master Putnam's oldest farm horse. Mercy was well beyond Ingersoll's when she took to the path again. There were rustling sounds behind her. Twigs cracked. Someone shuffled through dried leaves. She stopped to listen, and the sounds stopped. When she went on, the rustlings started. Indians? No. They moved silently through the forest on moccasined feet. It must be a large animal that was following her through the woods. She began to run again, making so much noise herself that she couldn't hear whether someone was running behind her.

She ran until she had a crick in her side and had to stop and lean against a tree. There was no sound at all. She looked back, and her cheek scraped against the rough bark of the tree, and it hurt. It was one of those moments when she felt so sorry for herself that she could have cried.

There was nothing to be seen or heard. The trodden path curved off out of sight beyond a great pine tree. The silence was more frightening than the sounds of movement. She thought, This forest goes on forever and forever. Who knows what lives in its dark, mysterious depth? Perhaps a demon lived there, and his voice would presently sound like thunder, calling, Mercy Lewis, Mercy Lewis, Mercy Lewis. She covered her ears with her mittened hands, for she had almost convinced herself that she would hear her name called out by some hideous demon that the wild Indians said their prayers to.

When she started out again, she followed the path. She tried to walk so quietly that no twigs snapped under her feet, no leaves rustled. Suddenly something grabbed her from behind. She had heard no footsteps, nothing. She recognized the iron grip of Pim's hand. She screamed, thinking that with hands like that he must have been apprenticed to a blacksmith. He's been playing hide-and-seek with me here in the woods—and she threw her head back and screamed again.

"Scream until you choke yourself," he said. "Nobody'll hear. I want my cards."

"I haven't got them."

"Where are they?"

Before she could answer, he said, "Don't tell me any more lies about the parson having them." He twisted her arm warningly.

"I never said he had them. I said they were at his house."

He twisted her wrist, and she screamed. "Scream till you choke," he said. "Where are my cards?"

"Abigail Williams, the minister's niece, has them."

"How'd she get them?"

"She took them away from me. She kept them."

"Kept them for what?" He twisted her wrist again.

"Tituba can tell fortunes. She's going to tell our fortunes."

"Tituba?" he said. "John Indian's wife?"

She nodded, and he said, "She can tell fortunes?"

"Yes." Mercy's hands were suddenly freed, and she began to rub her wrists.

"I still want my cards back, understand? You get those cards or don't ever come in Ingersoll's ordinary again. Not ever." He suddenly pushed her cloak aside, reached under it, and pinched the soft flesh of her upper arm. "Go ahead. Scream," he said and pinched her again. "I can box ears just as good as your mistress, and I'll lay in wait for you, and when you come through these woods, I'll box your ears, and I'll cut a switch and I'll—"

Mercy didn't scream again. Her eyes filled with tears. She didn't make a sound. The tears simply brimmed over, and big drops slid down her roughened cheeks.

"Oh," he said, disconcerted, and moved away from her, frowning. "Don't cry. Here." He sopped up her tears with a dirty piece of cloth that he pulled out of the pocket of his leather breeches. Then he bent forward and kissed her.

The carrot-colored hair, the flushed face, the firm, warm lips close to hers startled her so that she stopped crying.

"I won't hurt you any more," he said. "But please get my cards. They're the only thing I really own. Even these clothes—they're not mine. If I should run away, they'd say, 'Run away, the bound boy from Deacon Ingersoll's,' and they'd say I was wearing his clothes." He lowered his voice. "I've been thinking about running away, but I needed somebody to kind of look ahead and see what things would be like for me and where I ought to go. If Tituba can tell fortunes, she could tell me."

"Could I go with you when you run off?"

He looked at her doubtfully. "Two runaways from one place and one of them a girl? They'd catch us sure."

There was an embarrassed silence. He said, "You'll get my cards for me, Mercy?"

She nodded. She never thought she'd like him; he'd been so hateful, she'd been afraid of him. But now—she would keep thinking about that blazing red hair practically in her face, that gentle kiss, the sound of his voice when he said why he wanted his cards back and how desperately he wanted to know what the future held—

"Yes," she said softly. "I'll get them for you."

They went in opposite directions. He went towards Ingersoll's, and she went towards the minister's house. She kept thinking, Abigail is smaller than I am, younger than I am. I'll get the cards from her. Pinch me, will she? I can pinch, too. She stopped and pulled off a mitten and practiced on a fold of the coarse linsey-woolsey of her skirt, turning it, grabbing it between her fingers, and then turning the fingers, thinking, And the flesh will turn, too, and it will hurt, and I will get Pim's cards.

Her fingers were freezing cold, and she put her mitten back on. The places on her arm where Pim had pinched her would hurt for two or three days. They hurt the way a mark of the devil would hurt, or so Mistress Putnam had told her.

Afterwards she wished she'd stayed home, not gone to the minister's house that day. A dreadful thing happened there, and she didn't get the cards. She forgot them.

When she entered the keeping room of the minister's house and saw that Goody Good and her child, Dorcas, were there, she started to leave. Usually there was a good smell in the room. It came from the bundles of dried herbs hanging from the rafters and from whatever Tituba was cooking in the black pot over the fire. Goody Good's smell overlaid the other odors. Almost everybody thought she was a witch. She looked like one with that matted gray hair over her face, ragged clothes, and an ugly-smelling pipe.

Anne Putnam was there, too, and Anne said, "Oh, Mercy, I'm so glad you came. I do not like going through the woods alone. We can go home together."

Mary Walcott was sitting on one of the settles, knitting. She was always knitting. She was a close-by neighbor of the minister's, so she was always running in and out of the house. Horse-faced Mary Warren was sitting at the trestle table. Mercy looked at her and thought, She's like a big, slow-moving work horse. The talk was that her Master Proctor worked her like a horse. Goody Proctor was said to be delicate. Elizabeth Hubbard who did all the work at Dr. Griggs's house was at the table, too. She was an orphan, and though she was Mrs. Griggs's niece, she always looked so pinched and thin and scared that Mercy wondered just how well they treated her.

Mercy sat down on the settle near Betsey, thinking, I'll

wait until some of them go home, and pretty soon Abigail will go outdoors, and then I'll catch her and pinch her and get the cards from her. Abigail was sitting at the table, too, eyes sparkling, cheeks flushed as though she were excited.

But it wasn't like that at all. Abigail did not have the cards. Good had them. She took them from somewhere in her layers of rags and placed them on the trestle table.

"I want my fortune," she said.

Tituba said, "First return the gold chain."

Good reached inside her dress and took out a fine gold chain. She flung it at Abigail and it went on the floor. Tituba said, "Pick it up, Abigail, and put it away."

When Abigail came back into the room, Tituba said, "All right—now the cards."

Tituba unwrapped them, examined them, counted them.

"They're clean," Good said. "I wrapped 'm in a clean cloth, and they're all there. I kept 'm out of sight."

Mercy moved over to the table to watch.

Tituba shuffled the cards, laid them out. The first card that turned up was the hanged man, and Tituba frowned and shook her head.

"What's wrong?" Good asked, leaning forward.

"Something to eat," Dorcas said.

"Be quiet," Tituba ordered. "I'll get you something to eat, but you'll have to stay quiet. When I begin to read the cards, think about them but don't say anything. Don't ask any questions. Wait until I've finished."

"Why?" Mercy Lewis asked.

"Because it breaks the spell," Abigail said.

Breaks the spell? Mercy thought, troubled. Tituba can cast spells? She must have unusual powers if she can do that. Where does she get this power from? She followed Tituba over to the fire, curious as to what she was going to give Dorcas to eat. She noticed that Dorcas was holding a little doll-like figure in her hand. She was sitting on the settle close to the fire. The doll looked as though it had been made from an ear of corn with the shucks left on. It had cornsilk for hair, and a bit of dirty linen formed the skirt. Dorcas was bent over the doll, and she was sticking thorns in it with a fierceness that suggested she enjoyed what she was doing.

Tituba gave the child a piece of johnnycake and picked up the doll. Mercy looked at it, too. She saw that the doll looked rather like a child. The face and eyes and nose and mouth had been skillfully drawn with a piece of charcoal.

"Who made the dolly for you?" Tituba asked.

"Me mother."

"What's the dolly's name?"

Dorcas beckoned Tituba to come close and whispered, "Patience Mulenhorse."

"Why are you sticking thorns in your dolly?"

Mercy thought, It's not a dolly. It's a puppet. She was so frightened she felt sick. This was what witches did, made a figure to represent somebody and then stuck pins or thorns in it, and then the person sickened and died.

The child beckoned to Tituba again and whispered, "Won't tell."

Tituba put the puppet back on the settle and sat down at the table, shuffled the cards again and laid them out. She studied them for a long time. She pursed her lips, shook her head, and picked up the cards. She divided them into two sections, shuffled each section separately, and laid them out on the table. She kept frowning as though she were dissatisfied. She divided the cards in three sections, shuffled each section separately, and laid them out on the table again.

Finally she said, "There is death in the cards. You must leave Salem Village. Go somewhere else to live."

Good thrust her face almost into Tituba's. "What kind of stinking fortune is that to tell anybody? Leave the place where they live?"

"You don't live anywhere," Anne Putnam said. "You sleep in barns and in haystacks."

"If you stay in the Village," Tituba said, "you will be hanged."

Goody Good jumped up and swept all the cards off the table onto the floor. She took one leap across the room and grabbed Dorcas by the arm. "Those are the devil's cards," she shouted. "The devil's cards in the devil's house."

"It's all there in the cards," Tituba said calmly. "Three times I've shuffled, and three times I've laid them out. You watched me. And three times the Hanged Man was the first card I turned up. You saw it."

"Curse on you," Good shouted. She snatched Dorcas off the settle. "Curse on this house and all within—"

She left the door wide open behind her. As she went down the path she turned and bared her blackened teeth at them just like a wolf.

Mercy felt a shiver go down her spine. She couldn't swallow her own spittle. It was a frightening thing to be cursed like that. She watched Tituba pick up the cards, her dark-skinned hands moving so swiftly that in no time at all they were neatly stacked in a pile on the table. She could spin a fine strong thread, linen or woolen, so fast it seemed as if it wasn't done by human hands. She could find herbs near the roots of a tree, hands feeling around the root, head on one side as though she were listening to some voice nobody else could hear.

Mercy tried to say, "Give me the bound boy's cards," and no words came out. She felt the outside of her throat, and it felt as though it had swollen, increased in size. It seemed to her that the words wouldn't come out of her mouth, were stuck inside her throat, and were swelling up in there.

Tituba let the door stay open to air out the room. It got colder and colder inside. Finally she closed the door.

Abigail said, "Ugh! It still smells like Good in here. No wonder. Her child dropped the dolly. That's why the room still smells." She threw the cornhusk doll far back into the fire. It blazed up suddenly. Thick black smoke blew back into the room.

Mercy thought the face had twitched in the flame as though it were alive. There was a sound—Mercy heard it just as plain—a queer quick sound of protest.

Abigail said, horrified, "It cried out. The dolly cried out."

"That was Betsey," Tituba said sharply.

Betsey was staring at the fire, shaking and trembling. She began to cry. "How dreadful. The little child was burned up."

Abigail turned on her, shouting, "Don't you dare say that."

They all began to talk at once, filling the keeping room with their cries of protest, their accusations and denials.

Then the room was suddenly quiet because the Reverend Parris came home. Mercy wondered if he really thought they sat quiet like this when he was out of the room. Mary Walcott was knitting. All the rest of them were sitting down, their long gowns covering their feet, their hands folded in their laps.

He stood in front of the fire, warming his hands. He told them that a six-year-old child had been burned to death. She had gone to stir one of the big iron pots which hung from a lug pole in the chimney at the Ingersolls'. The lug pole broke and the child lost her balance and fell into the fire. It had happened just a little while ago.

There was a terrible stillness in the room.

"Whose child was it, Mr. Parris?" Mercy asked, remembering the puppet made of an ear of corn, the dried silk looking like dark brown hair, the face drawn to look like a child's face, the thorns stuck deep into the dolly's body.

"The Mulenhorse child. It was not steady on its feet, at best. It had been having fits and spells, and it had complained of being pricked and pinched. The mother thought the child had been overlooked by a witch."

"What was the child's name, master?" Tituba asked.

"Patience. Patience Mulenhorse."

"Well, why don't you say something?" Abigail demanded. "I know what you're thinking—" and she screamed. Betsey fell off the settle and lay insensible on the floor. Abigail began to run around the room, running in circles, around and around. It made Mercy dizzy to try to follow her; she had to keep turning her head.

Then Abigail ran straight towards the fire, shrieking, "I'll burn myself up. I'll burn myself up."

It took all of them to hold her back. Tituba slapped her very hard, and she quieted. It was quite a while before Betsey regained her senses. Tituba held her in her arms and talked to her and crooned to her.

On the way home, Anne Putnam clung tight to Mercy. Anne rode behind her on the horse, holding on to her. They were shivering and shaking. Their teeth chattered. They talked in whispers saying that they felt hot and then again that they felt cold. They didn't dare talk about what had happened at the minister's house.

Mercy kept wondering, What have we done? Have we raised some evil spirit from the dead? Anne had put that bright coin in the bottom of the bowl of water, but we all kept telling Betsey to look in the water, look in the water. We knew she'd go off in a trance. I wanted to talk to Mr. Burroughs' wives and Anne Putnam wanted to talk to her Aunt Bayley—

She made her thoughts shift back to the Mulenhorse child who had burned up in the fire. This had happened before, especially in winter. Sooner or later the sapling in the chimney that held the hooks for the pots would char all the way through. And then it would break. It wasn't the first time it had happened. It wouldn't be the last. It didn't mean anything—

Ah, she thought, but the dolly cried out. I heard it. Then she thought, I'll tell Pim that Tituba has his cards. I'll tell him to go to Tituba and get his fortune told.

Chapter 13

ERCY LEWIS woke up in the middle of the night. It was so dark she couldn't see the room at all. It was so cold she knew the backlog must have burned all the way through. She lifted her head and looked towards the fireplace. Yes, nothing left but a red glow.

I'll have to get up and put a log on the fire, but it's too cold to move. Even with a pile of quilts over her, she was cold. She could hear the wind howling outside. She lay there, not moving, feeling sorry for herself. She had a half-sick mistress and Anne, who wasn't much for cooking and cleaning, was no help. Mercy had to do all the indoors work. Fortunately Anne and her mother didn't eat much.

At least the Putnams weren't mean about firewood. Some places she'd been they were very mean. When she worked for the Reverend Burroughs he practically counted each stick as it went on the fire, froze himself and his wife and his children. Strong he was, too. He could lift a cask of molasses by himself. A short man. Very dark. Black hair. Black eyes. His eyes were like Good's—shiny, alive, the expression malicious.

If he had a religion she couldn't imagine what it was

like. Certainly not like other people's. She always thought of him as the little black minister. Well, he wasn't black like Tituba, but with his black clothes and dark hair and eyes and swarthy skin, the name suited him.

Once he found her in his study, looking at one of his books, and he shook her till her teeth hit against each other inside her head, and he boxed her ears so hard she heard a ringing sound in them for a month after.

Suddenly there was a sound she didn't recognize; she heard it under the wind. She called out, "Master Putnam, Master Putnam." She didn't expect a reply, and there was none.

She didn't dare move. It sounded as though someone or something was tapping on the kitchen window. The window was high up from the ground—how could they reach it? And what was it?

She lay shivering under the heavy quilts. Even if she shouted, the Putnams wouldn't hear her. Then there was a knocking at the door—and whoever or whatever it was knocked gently—ta-ta-ta-*tah*, ta-ta-ta-*tah*. Again and again. The rhythm of the bound boy's song echoed in her mind: Let the world *slide*, let the world *go*. Pim was at the door. She was sure of it.

She raised the big wooden bar, lifted the latch, and opened the door just a crack. Pim pushed the door open and came in, bringing a cold blast of air with him. He laid a bundle down on the settle, and she knew instantly that he was running away.

"You're going tonight?"

"Yes. And you can come with me. I've figured out how to do it."

"Why've you got to go so soon?"

"Because Tituba read my cards. She laid them out three times, and each time the cards said the same thing, that if anything happened that was strange, I was to leave right away."

He paused and lowered his voice, "And this afternoon—"

"You don't have to whisper. Can't none of 'em hear you. I thought Indians was raiding one night, and I screamed till I thought my throat would burst open. Nobody heard me. Just as well because there weren't a raid. Just branches against the windows."

When he started to say something, she said, "Wait. I got to fix the fire, or we'll freeze to death." He helped her pile logs on, and he used the bellows on it until there was a big roaring fire, and the room began to get warm, and it was filled with a cheerful yellow light from the fire.

She said, "What happened this afternoon?"

"That Abigail Williams, the parson's niece—she came to the ordinary. She and her cousin Betsey Parris, and they fell down in fits, and Abigail tried to crawl in the fire. I tried to hold her back, and I couldn't. It took me and John Indian and Goody Ingersoll and three men, strangers to me, to hold her down. She was hollerin' and screamin' and crying out, 'I'll ride him down, I'll ride him down,' and acting like she was a horse. Then she yelled, 'I'll not sign, old witch. I'll not sign the book,' and shrieked so it hurt my ears. Then Betsey Parris fell down unconscious, with froth and foam at her mouth. Then the other one began to dance, jumping up and down in one place till I thought she'd drop. And her tongue hung out of her mouth so far it near touched the floor."

"What was the matter with them?"

Pim made his face stern, pulled at an imaginary beard, and Mercy thought his beard would be bright red when he had one and it would tickle any girl who kissed him. The thought surprised her because it seemed to just pop into her head out of nowhere. Pim stood with his legs far apart, rocked back and forth, looked very thoughtful, and still pulling at an imaginary beard said, "It is possible that an evil hand be on them," and he laughed.

"It's not to laugh at," she said soberly.

"Well, some of the men in the tavern said they'd been overlooked by a witch. Does that sound better?" Then he said, "Who cares what they say? You said that when I went you wanted to go with me. So I've got boys' clothes in the bundle for you. You'll have to wear 'em. I can chop off your hair and no one will know you're a girl. I even brought along a scissors."

"My hair?" she said, touching her cap with a protective gesture. My hair? her mind echoed. She knew her face wasn't pretty, not really. The eyes were too small, and the nose turned up at the end, and her mouth was too wide. But her hair was pretty—long and thick and yellow as saffron.

"Well, I don't know—I don't rightly know."

"You can help me fix myself up while you make up your mind. Tituba gave me some dye from the black walnuts to darken my hair. She said it would be easy to find me with this red hair, but not so easy if the color was changed."

He untied his bundle. He took a flask out of it and a little wad of wool yarn. "You can do it better than I can," he said. He sat down on a stool right in front of the fire. "Wet the wad of yarn and then daub it on my hair. Don't get it on my face if you can help it because it takes a long time to get it off."

It was like magic. The thick red hair began to turn a deep dark brown as she daubed it with the dye. When she finished, his hair was dark brown, almost black. He didn't look like the same person. It frightened her. How did Tituba come to know so much? She even knew how to change a person's looks.

"Have you finished?" he asked impatiently.

"Yes. You don't look the same. You—"

"Good. You're next." He took a pair of leather breeches and a coarse rough shirt out of his bundle, and tossed them on the settle. "Put 'em on. No, first your hair. Here, sit down—" He patted the stool in front of the fire. "Sit right here."

"I don't want my hair cut."

"If you're going with me, I got to cut your hair. You've got to look like a boy. Sit down." He pulled her by the arm and pushed her down on the stool. He got a pair of scissors out of his bundle and clicked them together. "Take off your cap and undo your hair."

She took her hair down. It reached way below her waist. He cut it quickly, chopping it off. Long thick strands of yellow hair fell to the floor. He talked while he hacked at it.

"If it isn't safe for me here in the Village, then it isn't safe for you either. No matter what happens here, we'll be blamed for it. You watch and see. If the chimney catches on fire, why it's the bound boy's fault. If the cat eats the butter, it's the bound boy's fault. If the eggs can't be found, it's the bound boy's fault. Something's going to happen here. Tituba says all the signs point to it."

He gave a sigh of relief, "There, you're all done."

It was a frightening experience to have her hair cut. Her head felt light as though a weight had been removed. She'd keep those long thick strands of yellow hair, keep it with her, and she could braid it carefully and wind it around her head. When they got to wherever they were going, she could fix it on her head under her cap, and no one would ever know it had been cut off. She touched her head gently. It felt very queer, and she must look all naked just like a sheep that had had its fleece cut off. Pim was picking up the hair very carefully.

One moment she was sitting there fingering those short rough ends of hair, and the next thing she knew, there was a crackling in the fire. She turned to see what would burn fast and hot like that, and she was so furious she couldn't speak. It was her hair, her pretty yellow hair. Pim had bundled it up and thrust it in the fire, and it was burning, making a great hot blaze. In no time there was nothing left of it but little black things like beads and a smell as of something cooking—meat roasting on a spit or feathers burning. And her head felt hot—her hair burning like that right in front of her made her feel as though her head had been thrown in the fire.

She let out a cry, low, penetrating, and she turned on Pim, and went for his face and eyes, scratching him. He was so startled that he didn't defend himself, and she scratched both his cheeks.

He got hold of her hands and held them in his iron grip. "What is the matter with you?" he said with a hiss.

"My hair," she whispered. She tried to shriek and only a whisper came out. "You've burned my hair."

"What were you going to do with it? Carry it around with you? It would be a dead give-away, a boy travelin' around with that big wad of yellow hair. Haven't you any sense?" He let go of her hands and shook her and then thrust her away from him.

"You burned my hair. It was all I had." She could hardly talk. "You go. I won't go with you. You're mean—"

"I'm not mean," he protested. "I'm—well, I know it isn't going to be easy for me to get clean away. With you along it's even harder. But this way they'd be fooled. They'll be looking for a redheaded boy and a girl. We'll be two boys—one with dark hair. It would give us a little more time."

She felt of her head, it seemed to have shrunk in size. The hair felt rough, uneven. Her head was cold. It was a terrible thing to lose a part of you that you'd had ever since you could remember, have part of you burned up right before your eyes. His hands had been hard, unfriendly, as they hacked off her pretty yellow hair.

"Here," he said, just as though he hadn't heard a word she said. He held out the leather breeches. "Put the breeches on."

She shook her head, and the short, unevenly cut hair fell forward, covering her face. She pushed it away impatiently. "No," she repeated, "I'll not go with you."

He put the breeches back in his bundle along with the little wad of yarn, the flask, and the scissors. He said, frowning, "If I get caught, I'll know you told on me. I'll make you pay for it, Mercy Lewis. If you tell I was here, I'll—"

"But my hair," she said. "What'll folk say when they see my hair?"

"Tell 'em a devil did it. Tell 'em you fought all night with the devil. Here, I'll turn over the trestle table and upend the stools." He turned them over quickly and noisily, and he began to laugh. "Where do you keep the Indian meal?" He opened a press cupboard, rummaged through it. "Ah, this'll do"—as he scattered corn meal all over the floor—"Tell 'em you fought a pitched battle with the devil with Deacon Putnam's weevily corn meal."

He picked up his bundle and came towards her, scowling, "If you tell—" he began.

There were slow heavy footsteps from somewhere in the front of the house. "Hurry," she said, "Deacon Putnam's coming—" She unbarred the door for him. "I'll not tell."

"Tell the old psalm-sayer there was a demon here. Leave the door open—"

When Deacon Putnam entered the kitchen, Mercy was sitting by the fire, her head between her knees, the short yellow hair dangling down. She looked as though she had been beheaded.

"I heard voices, Mercy," Deacon Putnam said. "The door is open"—he closed it—"and this big fire going. Who was here?"

She moaned, and then she screamed. When he touched her on the shoulder, she jumped up, away from him, crying out, "You devil—you devil," sobbing and covering her face with her hands. "What else do you want? I'll not sign. You can cut the rest of my hair straight back to my scalp, and I'll not sign your book—"

Deacon Putnam said, "There are no devils here, Mercy. It is I, your master, Deacon Putnam."

She took her hands away from her face, looked at him to see if he believed her. His expression was one of astonishment. He kept looking around the room, at the overturned benches and stools, at the long trestle table that had been turned upside down, at the corn meal scattered all over the floor. He leaned over and picked some of it up, rubbing it between his fingers.

"I didn't think anyone would ever come," she sobbed. She had never seen him in his bedclothes before. He had on a nightcap and a thick woolen bedgown. He looked shorter and wider than when he was wearing his day clothes.

"There, there," he said, patting her shoulder. "What happened? Tell me about it."

She said that a demon had entered the room. He had an old woman with him. She didn't know how they got in; she awakened, and they were there. They pulled her off the settle and threatened her, saying that she must worship the demon as if he was God. He kept putting a book in her hand. He said she must sign it, and when she refused, he said he'd cut off her head, and he'd start with her hair. He piled fresh logs on the fire until it was a big roaring fire—flames going up the chimney so high she was sure he was trying to burn the house down.

The old woman had held her down while he hacked off all her hair and then he'd burned it. Afterwards he'd walked up and down in front of the fire, hands behind his back, sneering at her and saying, "Feel the fire, Mercy? Feel it on your head?" He had a slight limp when he walked because he had a shoe on his right foot but his left leg ended in a cloven hoof.

Just in telling it, she got so upset that she began to sob again and to cry out, and she ran towards the fire, and Deacon Putnam had to hold her back, and he shouted for help. Mistress Putnam and Anne, Jr., came running into the room, in their nightcaps and shifts. This made her scream even louder. They slept in feather beds, and they had special clothes to sleep in. She slept in the same coarse linsey-woolsey dress that she worked in, slept fitfully, curled up on that hard narrow settle.

When Anne Putnam, Jr., heard the story, heard about the devil who had cut off Mercy's hair and burned it, she started to shiver and to shake. When Mercy said, "I could feel my head burning," she let out a small scream.

Anne Putnam, Jr., suddenly said, "What's that?" pointing to Mercy's hand.

Mercy looked, too. Her fingertips were a dark, dark brown, almost black. Some of the walnut stain she'd used on Pim's red hair had stained her fingers. She did not know what to say so she began to tremble and shake and moan and wring her hands, saying that her head felt cold and that she was afraid.

Deacon Putnam said, "The child said the demon wanted her to sign his book. He probably held her hand on it and thus it was blackened, just from touching it. Is that right, Mercy?"

She nodded and said, "I wouldn't sign. I wouldn't sign

and I kept saying so—." She thought, Sixteen years old I am and up until now I have been the serving wench. That's what they've always called me and now, now, I am a child to be treated tenderly.

Anne Putnam, Jr., began to cry. "I am afraid, too," she sobbed. "I am afraid, too."

After the Putnams got them both quieted, Mistress Putnam said, "Come, Mercy"—and her voice was kind and compassionate—"you sleep with Anne for the rest of the winter. Tomorrow we will make some shifts for you, so you will have proper clothes for a bed."

It was very soft and very warm in Anne Putnam's feather bed. Mercy thought it was almost as though the feathers surrounded you. If you lay on your back, your back was warm and your sides were warm, because you sank way down in the feathers. She'd helped make this feather tick for Anne's bedframe. The feathers had been most carefully selected, and there had been a great many of them because it had to be extra thick so it would be extra warm.

They were covered by a patchwork quilt, and on top of that there was a thick bearskin rug, the fur side down. She stretched out, full length, and then turned and lay on her side. Part of her front, part of her back were warmed by the feather bed. The bearskin rug warmed the rest of her. When she slept on the narrow wooden settle, it had been in snatches. She had turned and twisted all night long, afraid she would fall off, always cold, and the settle hard and unyielding.

She sighed and settled deep into the warm, soft bed. She pulled the bearskin high up around her neck and finally covered her head because she could feel cold air all around her shorn head. Tomorrow night she'd wear one of Anne Putnam's nightcaps. Just before she drifted off to sleep, she decided that this deep, soft, warm bed was better than life with the bound boy would have been. The Putnams were always saying, "Better one bird in hand than ten in the wood."

She dreamed that she was in the woods and that a little yellow bird kept fluttering in front of her, and she twisted and turned to get away from it because the yellow bird is the Devil's bird. Everybody knows that.

Chapter 14

Tituba was preparing the noon meal. She was stirring the contents of an iron pot that was hanging over the fire. To her surprise, John came hurrying into the keeping room. She had never seen him so excited since they had lived in Salem Village.

He said Pim, the bound boy at Ingersoll's, had run away and taken four silver spoons, two sets of leather breeches, one pair never worn, Deacon Ingersoll's finest musket, and all the kitchen knives.

He stopped talking, caught his breath, said, "What would he want with kitchen knives?"

"He could sell them in Boston."

"And Mercy Lewis—Mercy Lewis—" Here the words tumbled out, one right after another, so fast that Tituba had trouble understanding him. "A devil cut off her hair last night. An old woman and a devil cut off her hair right in Deacon Putnam's keeping room—"

"What?" Tituba said, and then she frowned. "An old woman? What old woman? How did they get in the house?"

"Come right through the door as though it weren't

there. And when the devil gave Mercy his book to sign and she wouldn't sign it, why the old woman held her down—a very strong old woman she was. And the devil cut off Mercy's long yellow hair while he held her by the neck with one of his horny hands."

Tituba tried to say, "Where—"

John held up his hand, "Wait. I have to tell it all at one time, or I'll forget some of it. Where was I? Oh, Deacon Putnam woked up, what with the noise and confusion, the devil's loud hoarse shouts, and Mercy Lewis' screams, and the old woman's coarse voice, and the sounds of the struggle—the trestle table knocked over, the stools knocked over, as the devil and the old woman wrestled with Mercy Lewis, holding her, cutting her hair, hacking it off—and then—what then?"

"Deacon Putnam came in?"

"Yes, yes. And the room was filled with the smell of sulphur and brimstone, and the door was wide open, and poor little Mercy sat there on a stool in front of the fire, her head hung over her knees, her yellow hair all short and rough cut. Deacon Putnam said his finest Indian meal was strew all over the floor."

"No great loss," Tituba said. "Deacon Putnam's meal is always full of weevils. Everybody knows that. How did the meal get on the floor?"

"Mercy Lewis threw it at the devil. After he cut her hair, she kept the devil away from her by throwing Indian meal at him."

Tituba said, laughing, "John, do you believe that?"

"That's what she said," he answered. "She said she kept throwing that Indian meal at the demon by the handful and shouting, 'The whole armor of God be between you and me!' "

Tituba shook her head. "I think she's having sport with the Putnams. When did Deacon Ingersoll find out that Pim was gone?"

"First thing this morning. No fire in the kitchen. No wood brought in. No stock been fed. No cows been milked. They look in the lean-to. Not there. They look in the root cellar. Not there. Look everywhere. Not there. Deacon Ingersoll says, 'Count everything.' Spoons is gone. Gun is gone. New leather breeches is gone. Old leather breeches is gone. Redheaded boy is gone, too."

Though John did not say so, Tituba knew he was quoting Cow John, the old man with the harelip who looked after the Putnam's big herd of cows.

"I hope he gets away free and clear," she said. "A young strong fellow like that should be his own master."

John nodded in agreement. "Deacon Ingersoll says he had a bad influence on all the bound boys and girls for miles around. He was always singing that song about he didn't give a fig for this and he didn't give a fig for that. Deacon says he thought from the first time he saw him that only an imp of Satan would have had hair that color."

"His hair was that color when Deacon Ingersoll got him in Boston. Why did he bring him here if he thought he belonged to Satan?"

"He didn't have to pay much for him. Nobody would bid on him because of the color of his hair, and the captain of the *Blessing* wanted to get rid of him."

John said he had to hurry back. More and more people

would be coming into the taproom as the story about Mercy Lewis' fight with a demon spread through the Village. They would come in hope they'd hear Mercy tell her story and catch a glimpse of her shorn head. He hoped he'd see it himself.

Late in the afternoon, Mercy Lewis came to see Tituba. She had a shawl over her head and refused to take it off. Tituba thought she looked older and very pale and tired.

When Abigail came downstairs and saw Mercy, she said, "Let me see what the demon did to you."

Mercy shook her head and held the dark brown shawl tight around her throat. Abigail snatched it off, snatched off Mercy's cap, and stared at the shorn head. Mercy's hair was all short lengths and it had obviously been hacked off. No effort had been made to cut it evenly. It was a shocking sight.

Mercy put the shawl over her head, in silence, and left. Tituba followed her outside and put her hand on her arm, detaining her.

"It was Pim who cut your hair?"

Mercy nodded, head down, eyes on the ground, refusing to look at Tituba. She said that he wanted her to run away with him, dressed as a boy, and she might have gone but he threw her hair into the fire and the sight of her hair burning and the smell of it frightened her. Deacon Putnam was on his way into the room, and Pim told her to say a devil had cut off her hair.

"Was there an old woman with him?"

"No. I just said that so folk would wonder which woman in Salem Village had sold her soul to the devil. It would give them something else to talk about. You'd probably 've done the same. I heard a crackling noise, and it was my hair burning and flaming up. And my head felt hot. And there were places on my neck felt cold, where the scissor touched against the skin. It was like having your neck cut off from your head and your head burned up all at the same time. And next thing there was Master Putnam saying, 'I heard voices. Who was here?' "

She looked down at the snow, and then she looked at Tituba. "I should have gone with Pim. He's free to go where he wants, and I'm still bound even though the Putnams do let me sleep in the same bed with Anne, Jr." Then she lowered her voice, "Did you give him back his pretty cards?"

"Yes."

"He said you told his fortune. What was it like?"

"It was a fine fortune. He will go round the world. And some day he will be rich."

Mercy began to cry. "I should have gone with him," she sobbed, and fell down in the snow. Her shawl came off her head, and her cap came off, too. She lay there, motionless, tears streaming down her cheeks, the unevenly cut hair as yellow as buttercups against the snow. Finally she began to scream, and she had a screaming fit just like Abigail's fits.

After that she had them quite often. So did Anne Putnam, Jr. Sometimes they thought they were dogs, and they barked and ran around on all fours. Sometimes they thought they were cats, and they mewed and hissed. Then again they thought they were geese, and they ran across the floor, their feet scarcely touching, and they flapped their arms as though they were wings.

John told Tituba that Mercy Lewis and Anne Putnam, Jr., were like a stage play in the taproom. Many farmers were coming from the outlying districts to watch them.

Tituba said, "The farmers come here, too. They bring provisions for the minister. Then they wait to see if Abigail will have a fit. Sometimes there are three or four of them sitting lined up on the settle."

Abigail's fits got so bad and occurred so often that the master sent for Dr. Griggs. He put his ear to her chest and to Betsey's, looked in their eyes, peered down their throats. He shook his head.

Dr. Griggs came back every day for a week. He bled them. He gave them terrible-tasting medicines. The fits continued. Betsey's fits were not like Abigail's. She talked in a queer guttural voice and then slumped to the floor, unconscious. It wasn't always possible to understand what she said.

Finally Dr. Griggs said, "I think they are under an evil hand."

When he said this, the candle in the upstairs room flickered and went out, and a gust of smoke came down the chimney, setting them all to coughing. Puss, the money cat, ran under Tituba's skirt and stayed there.

The master looked frightened. He said it would be necessary to fast and hold a day of prayer.

The next afternoon the keeping room was crowded with people. Even the mistress was brought down from her upstairs bedroom to sit on the settle, wrapped in quilts. Abigail and Betsey were there. So were Deacon Putnam and his wife and Mercy Lewis and Anne Putnam, Jr., Goody Sibley and her niece Mary Walcott, Dr.

Griggs and Mrs. Dr. Griggs and their niece Elizabeth Hubbard. Horse-faced Mary Warren wasn't there. Master Proctor sent word that he was going to keep her at her wheel and thrash her if she dared leave it.

Tituba thought the master would never have done with praying. She was kneeling next to Abigail and slowly became aware that Abigail was growing more and more restless. She twitched whenever the Lord's name was mentioned. They said the Lord's prayer in unison. When they reached "hallowed be Thy name," Abigail screamed and screamed and fell down on the floor, crying and moaning and saying that she was being pinched and pricked with needles, that she was being choked. Tituba sponged off her face. She was surprised to find that Abigail had stiffened in a strange fashion. She gave her a spoonful of the medicine Dr. Griggs had left. Finally the girl was able to get up from the floor. She looked very well. Her cheeks were rosy. Her eyes sparkled.

But they had to stop praying. Abigail would not or could not kneel. She began running up and down the keeping room, weaving in and out between the benches and stools on which the people were seated. She ran to the fire, and before anyone could stop her, she reached in with the poker and poked out a burning log and started pushing it around the room.

People stood up, moved out of the way lest the sparks ignite their clothing. For a few moments they were too frightened to go near her—even Tituba was aghast.

Abigail shouted in a loud rude voice, "Way—way—make way. I am here now. I have come. I am here. Way —way—make way—"

The room was full of smoke. There was danger of fire, and still they stood and stared at her. Tituba thought, watching her, You could really believe she was bewitched. Abigail moved fast. When she was in the darkest parts of the big, low-ceilinged room you couldn't really see her. Her clothing was dark, and all you could see was the fiery log as she pushed it around. The log looked as though it were going around and around by itself.

It took the master and Deacon Ingersoll, Deacon Putnam, and Dr. Griggs to hold Abigail. She fought with them and struggled, kicked them, pushed her elbows in their sides.

Tituba took the tongs and put the log back in the fireplace. Then she seized a birch broom and hastily swept up bits of charred wood that were still smouldering, thinking, If the floor hadn't been heavily sanded, Abigail could have set the house on fire.

Mistress Parris was quietly weeping. Betsey had fallen on the floor, unconscious. Tituba picked Betsey up, cradled her in her arms, crooned to her, talked to her, and then laid her gently on the settle with her mother.

Deacon Ingersoll said, "They have been overlooked by a witch," in his high-pitched voice. Tituba thought he looked at her out of the corner of his eyes.

"They are under an evil hand," Dr. Griggs said.

Tituba noticed that Mercy Lewis looked startled and then covered her mouth with her hand, concealing her expression.

The master bowed his head and said harshly, "We must pray and fast and wait for a sign from the Lord."

Then all their visitors left at once. The women put on

their cloaks and wrapped their heads in shawls, and the men bundled themselves in their greatcoats, pushed their felt hats down on their heads, picked up their muskets, and hastened away. Tituba thought they hurried off the way people do when they are frightened.

She helped the mistress up the steep narrow flight of stairs, helped her to bed, covered her up. She freshened the fire in the mistress' room. She made certain the girls were in bed. Abigail looked fresh and rosy as she always did after she had one of her fits. Betsey was already asleep, and she had the pinched, white look of a truly sick person.

Tituba went downstairs, shielding the candle against drafts with one hand. She looked at her hand in the candlelight. It was a work-worn hand, the dark brown skin grayed and roughened, the fingers just a little out of shape at the joints. Was this an evil hand, she wondered, a hand that wove and cooked and spun and cleaned and gardened, a hand that milked cows and nursed a sick woman and cared for two children?

Had Dr. Griggs, that short, bustling little man, who knew so little about medicinals that he often consulted her as to what was the best way to treat boils and to cure fevers and chills or a running-off of the bowels—had he meant her? Was hers the "evil hand"?

Tituba began to wonder if Abigail's fits were contagious. Two days afterwards she learned that Elizabeth Hubbard now had fits like Abigail's, and so did Mary Warren and Mary Walcott.

John said he thought that Mercy Lewis and Anne Putnam, Jr., came to Ingersoll's ordinary just so people could see them taken in one of their fits. He said they crept under benches and stools, got under the settles. Sometimes they stayed there with their tongues hung way out. The Putnam girl screeched like an owl—only it was worse to listen to, higher and longer and louder. He began to feel that if he listened too long he'd go right out of his senses. Then he demonstrated what they did when they were having these terrible fits.

Tituba said she didn't think their behavior in the ordinary was any more astounding than what went on in the master's keeping room. Sometimes there would be five or six people who had brought onions or turnips or carrots to be entered in the rate book. Mercy Lewis and Anne Putnam, Jr., and Mary Walcott and Abigail would run around and around in the room. They shrieked that they were being pinched and bitten. Their heads were twisted around. Their eyes were rolled back. They said they were being frozen, and their faces whitened like corpses. Almost immediately they said they were being burned, and they turned a fiery red.

As in the ordinary, Abigail always supplied the most horrifying touch. She would run straight towards the fire, shouting, "I will burn! I will burn!" It took three or four strong men and one or two bound boys to hold her back.

Nothing like this had ever been seen in the Village. There was continual talk about witchcraft. There was fear mixed with the talk. People began to eye each other doubtfully. Nobody knew who the witch was. Nobody felt safe. Three more girls were now bewitched and having fits just like the others: Sarah Churchill, servant to

George Jacobs, and Elizabeth Booth and Susanna Sheldon, bound girls held by families in the neighborhood of Ingersoll's ordinary.

By the middle of February, John was so concerned that he came home from the ordinary every night in spite of storms and high drifted snow. He told Tituba he didn't like all this talk of witches and witchcraft. He said that for all their long, slow prayers and their long, slow sermons, these were a cold, cruel people. Though they believed in angels, they also believed in devils. They believed witches obtained their power from the Devil, the result of having signed a covenant with the Devil, having signed his book.

He said, "At Ingersoll's there is a constant cry, 'Find out the witch, find out the witch.' They quote from the Bible, 'Do not suffer a witch to live.' They will not be satisfied until they hang somebody. They talk of all the things that have gone wrong—and they go back for years —they tell of cows dying and horses refusing to move. They tell their dreams. They speak of huge cats that sit on their chests all night and will not let them move. They say these things happen because there's a witch in the Village."

"Why do you worry so?"

"Because in Boston I saw them hang the Witch Glover. She was nothing but an old crazy woman with matted hair and—"

He was silent, remembering. Then he said, "Our master lectures on witchcraft. He stands in the taproom, reads from a book by Cotton Mather: 'If David thought it a sad thing to fall into the hands of men, what is it, to fall into the hands of Devils? The hands of Turks, of Spaniards, of Indians, are not so dreadful as those hands that Witches do their works of Darkness by. O what a direful thing is it, to be pricked with pins and stabbed with knives all over, and to be filled all over with Broken bones—' " John's voice sounded exactly like the master's voice.

They were both silent, and then John said, "They think that unless they can find out who has bewitched the children, they will all die."

"Die?" Tituba asked. "Maybe some of them will. My little Betsey, perhaps, but not Abigail. She looks better after she's had a fit than she did before she had it. All these orphan nieces and bound girls come out of their fits, looking very lively. So does Anne Putnam, Jr. But not Betsey."

Betsey was growing thinner and paler and more frightened every day. On the other hand, Abigail flourished. Tituba tried to remember what she herself had been like at twelve, and shook her head. At twelve she could do almost as much hard work as a grown woman. She worked in the cookhouse on the plantation. She knew how to cook and to sew and how to clean a house and to weed a garden. When she was fourteen she was sold to Mistress Endicott.

Abigail had never learned to work steadily at something and finish it and do it well. She didn't want to help, and so did everything badly.

Poor little Betsey could not work at anything steadily either. Even before the seizures started, her mind wandered and her hands stopped working. If the cat sat up and washed his face, going over it carefully with his paw, pausing to moisten his paw with his tongue, Betsey stopped sewing to watch him. The thread would break, or she would lose the needle, or the thread would become knotted so badly that she had to discard it and start over. So she never finished anything.

If she were outdoors, her attention might be caught by a butterfly flitting among the flowers or by a worm slowly inching over the ground. She would absent-mindedly pull up weeds and plants, too, watching the long grass in the meadow. Sometimes she sat without moving because a brilliantly colored bird flew through the orchard and started singing, and she had to stay still so she could listen to the song.

Sometimes Tituba thought it would have been better if the master hadn't owned slaves. But with a sickly wife and two young children, how would he have managed?

Then she decided he could have managed if he'd had a young, strong woman to help. Abigail would have been so busy she wouldn't have had time to become bewitched, and little Betsey—Tituba sighed thinking about her. The poor child saw things in corners, talked in her sleep, cried too easily, laughed too easily. She was afraid of her father, afraid of Abigail. She loved her mother, but she was afraid she might die. Tituba was always aware, when she helped the mistress during one of those dreadful fits of coughing, that little Betsey was huddled in one corner of the room, eyes big with fear, small body shivering with fear. Sometimes she thrust her small, cold hand into Tituba's hand, whispering, "Don't let her die, Tituba. Don't let her die."

After John left, Tituba kept thinking of the phrase, "those hands that witches do their works of darkness by."

The next day she spoke to Goody Sibley about Betsey, pointing out how pitifully thin the child had grown, how easily startled she was.

Goody Sibley said, "She's bewitched. We have to find out who the witch is and break her power. I can find out."

"The girls don't know who bewitches them," Tituba said. "The master has asked Abigail, and Deacon Putnam has asked Mercy Lewis and Anne Putnam, Jr., and Dr. Griggs has asked Elizabeth Hubbard—they don't know."

"We'll find out," Goody Sibley said confidently. "I'll make a witch cake. I know how to do it. My mother gave me the recipe just before she died. We'll wait for a day when Mr. Parris is not home. I'll need John Indian to help me. We'll get all the bewitched girls together here in your keeping room, and we'll find out."

Tituba thought, Not all of them are girls. Only three of them could be called girls—Betsey is nine, and Abigail is twelve, and Anne Putnam, Jr., is twelve. But the others are young women. Mary Walcott, Elizabeth Hubbard, and Mercy Lewis are seventeen; Elizabeth Booth and Susanna Sheldon are eighteen, and Mary Warren and Sarah Churchill are twenty.

"You will want all of them?"

"No. Just the ones who were first bewitched. Betsey and Abigail and Anne Putnam and Mercy Lewis and Mary Walcott and Elizabeth Hubbard and Mary Warren. You'll see. The witch cake will draw the witch to the house."

Chapter 15

ON THE day that the Reverend Samuel Parris went to Boston to consult with the Boston clergy on how best to handle the matter of witchcraft in Salem Village, Goody Sibley made a witch cake.

She arrived at the minister's house soon after he left. She brought her niece, Mary Walcott, with her. She had a big bundle under her arm, and she put this down on the settle in the keeping room. She managed to pull her dog Ranter inside with her.

Ranter had barked indiscriminately at everything that moved along the road—birds, squirrels, even dried leaves blowing in the wind. When he entered the minister's dooryard and saw Tituba's money cat, he barked frantically. The money cat hissed at him and then went towards the woods with his tail up in the air.

And now Ranter was pleasantly excited and not inclined to stay inside a house.

"I've sent word to John Indian to come and help me," Goody Sibley explained, as she tied Ranter to the crossbar on the big door. "Anne Putnam, Jr., and Mercy Lewis and the others will be along soon."

"You don't have to tie the dog up," Tituba said.

"I'll need him later on."

Tituba said, frowning, wondering what was to happen to the dog, "Sometimes these strange old cures don't turn out right. I'm not sure we should do this."

Abigail said, "Oh, yes, we must do this."

By the time John arrived, the girls were all present and the witch cake had been made. Goody Sibley had mixed rye meal with the children's urine and poured it into a flat pan, ready to be thrust directly into the fire where it would bake when the time came. She said that John must get up on the roof and stop up the chimney.

"Stop up the chimney?" he said, perplexed. "All the smoke will come in the house. Why don't you put the fire out if you don't want a fire going?"

She shook her head. "No. There must be a fire in the fireplace so that I can bake the witch cake, but the opening into the chimney must be closed lest the witch escape up the chimney. Everything must be closed."

Tituba knew when he'd stopped up the chimney because smoke began to drift into the room. Then John came in and carefully closed the door behind him and barred it. The girls were watching with great interest—no sign of fits or sound of shrieks.

Goody Sibley undid her bundle. She put a long piece of black woolen cloth around her neck and put a hood of black lambskin on her head. She put more logs on the fire. She moved a pot of water closer to her. She then thrust the witch cake deep into the heart of the fire. Smoke poured out of the chimney. Tituba could barely see the blaze. She could barely see Goody Sibley crouched in front of the fire.

Goody Sibley began to rock back and forth, and she crooned, "O coom, great Kelah, coom, coom to the meal with seed of each gender, coom."

Tituba got the uneasy feeling that something had entered the room. They couldn't see each other because of the smoke. The girls were making choking sounds, and John was coughing. The dog began to whine and yelp and struggle to get free of the rope that held him.

Goody Sibley took the witch cake out of the fire, and as far as Tituba could tell, she sprinkled it with water from the black pot to cool it off. Then she and John thrust the dog's snout into it, and he gobbled it down, and Tituba wondered if there had been something added to the rye meal to make him wolf it down with such relish. Then John touched the dog under the tail, and she smelled oil of wintergreen. The dog yelped and jumped straight up in the air, and John cut the rope that had been holding him.

Tituba, not thinking what she was doing, eyes smarting and running, coughing, choking, ran to the door and opened it, and the dog went out of the house, leaping and yelping and running in circles in the snow. Tituba went outside, too, choking and coughing. Even though it was cold and she had no shawl around her, she stood outside taking deep breaths of the clean, cold air. It was a wonder they hadn't died shut up in that room with only smoke to breathe. She walked away from the house. Smoke was pouring out of the front door.

She caught a whiff of a familiar odor, rank, sour-smelling, and turned around. Goody Good was coming around the side of the house. She had Dorcas by the hand.

"I'm hungered," she whined. "Ye said I should leave the

Village. What kind of fortune was that to tell a body? I'm ye friend, Tituba. Dorcas and I are ye friends—" She broke off. "What crooked-handed woman is that?"

A horse had stopped in front of the house, and a young man was helping an old woman down from the horse. She stumbled when she got off the horse, and he held on to her, and then she gestured that he was to release her, and she came towards them; walking slowly.

"It's old Gammer Osburne," Goody Good said. "It's old Gammer Osburne. Probably looking for Minister. Folks say she's no Gospel woman. Hasn't set foot in meeting for three years. Not since she married the redemptioner." She peered at the woman. "Thought ye was bedrid."

"I came to see Tituba."

Good pointed at Tituba. "That's her. That's her. What d'ye want of her? She tells bad fortunes."

Gammer Osburne said, "They say you've got a tea made of iris root that stops pain and that you only give it to folk if they come for it. I came to ask you to give some of it to me."

Tituba said, "There was no need to come for it. You could have sent somebody. Come in now and rest yourself before you start for home." The skin on the woman's face was like the snow and pitted like snow that has started to melt.

Good said, "Is the house afire?"

"No. The chimney was stopped up and it's smoking."

"Ye sure ye want to set in that smoke, Gammer Osburne? Look at it pour out—ye sure the house ain't afire?"

"I have to rest," Osburne said. "It'll air out fast in this

cold clear weather, if you leave the door open for a while."

Tituba led the way, and Osburne stumbled on the stone step behind her. She turned to help her; Good got on the other side, and they went through the door together.

The girls turned towards them, round-eyed, not falling down in fits, but silent, staring.

Finally Abigail said, "It's Tituba. Tituba is the witch," and her breath came out in a long sigh.

Mercy Lewis said, "It's Goody Good. Good is a witch," and covered her eyes.

Mary Warren said, "It's my Aunt Osburne. Osburne is a witch—Osburne is a witch—" and she started to whinny like a horse.

"A plague on ye," Good shouted. "Who's a witch? Who says I'm a witch?"

"I do," Abigail said boldly. "All three of you are witches. You've bewitched us. Goodwife Sibley said that after the witch cake is baked and the dog eats it, right after that whoever comes into the house first—those are the witches. You came in all at once, all three of you together. You were drawn by the witch cake."

John shouted at Abigail. "Not the people who live here. Not Tituba. It is only natural that a person who lives in a place should enter it or return to it. Tituba isn't a witch—"

Good said, "Ye are a fine one to talk about witches. They tell me this one"—pointing at Betsey—"knows what's going to happen before it happens. If there be any witchcraft practiced, it's here, right here." She picked up the poker from the fireplace and pounded on the floor with it. "And if there be any witches in the Village," she said, her eyes blazing with anger, "they be here. They be ye, and ye, and ye—" And she pointed the poker at Abigail and Betsey and Mercy Lewis and Anne Putnam, Jr., and Mary Warren, each one in turn. Then she was taken with a fit of coughing from the smoke and had to stop.

Goody Osburne turned away from them and spoke directly to her niece, Mary Warren. Her voice trembled. "You'll come to no good end, miss, with this dabbling in the black art. You know I'm no witch. You spread lies and gossip about me and have ever since you've had to work for your keep."

She went off without the iris-root tea, hobbling out of the room without a backward glance.

Goody Sibley said, "John is right. Tituba lives here and—"

Abigail said, "You said whoever came through the door first, no matter who it was, was the witch or witches. Tituba and Good and Osburne came in together, all at the same time. They are the witches."

John said, eyes narrowed, "I will not listen to any more talk about Tituba being a witch."

Good said, "What about me? Who speaks for me?" There was silence, and she said, "I cursed ye before and I curse ye again. A rot, a pox, and a plague on ye—"

John went to unstop the chimney. They left the door open. The smoke began to go up the chimney.

Betsey said, "If Tituba is a witch, so am I—so am I."

There was an awkward silence in the room. Tituba said nothing.

Then they all went home. They were silent, white-faced as they left. John went back to Ingersoll's ordinary.

That night when he came home he said that the farmers and the fishermen were coming from as far as Ipswich and Salem, and folk were coming from Boston, in the hope of seeing some of the girls in their falling and screeching fits. All the rooms at the ordinary were taken, and there were folk in the taproom until quite late. He said that someone had said it was a strange thing that so many of these afflicted young women were orphaned nieces or bound girls or servants. He doubted that their owners got much work out of them any more, what with their choking fits and their falling fits and their screeching fits.

It was quiet in the keeping room. The smoke was all gone. There was nothing to indicate that a fresh-cheeked woman had baked a witch cake in the fireplace in the afternoon and that three women had been named as witches as a result. The fire made a soft, yellow light; it softened the outlines of the settles and the long trestle table.

John said, "They speak of you in the ordinary, and they speak of this house. And they speak of the master." He leaned against the corner of the settle, and she knew he was going to imitate the sound of the voices he had heard in the taproom.

He said, " 'I don't want a man for a minister who has witches in his house.' " Then he waited and said, " 'Even his daughter is a witch. . . . So is his niece. His niece can fly. I've seen her.'

" 'His slave is a witch.'

" 'Yes, she tells fortunes.' "

Three nights later, John said, in his own voice, "This is

not safe for us. In the tavern they keep saying, 'Do not suffer a witch to live.' They all know about the witch cake and what happened here. The master knows it, too. He is like a sly fox. He knows it, but he has said nothing. And then they tell these old stories about being struck dumb for days and days, and if somebody asks them when this was, why it happened ten years ago or five years ago."

The next night he said the same thing. "They keep telling stories about you. They forget that I'm married to you, or else they think I am deaf, for they speak of you in front of me."

The next morning, early, he was out in the barn with her, helping her feed the animals. He said that the night before two men were in the taproom. They said they had been going home, going through the woods, and they heard a strange noise, a noise they'd never heard before, and it continued so many times they were affrighted.

"I think I can tell it exactly the way I heard it," he said. " 'I be coming home at night and I keep hearing a noise, a strange noise. I never heard before. And it went on for so long I be afraid. But I kept going, and then I see a strange and unusual beast lying on the ground. Then there rose up from the ground the minister's slave Tituba, and Goody Good in her rags, and Goody Osburne all rheumy-eyed and coughing. It were almost like seeing cattle rise up out of a low place in the ground, and a man with them and a mist all about them.' "

John rubbed his forehead and let his breath out in a sigh. "But the part that—oh, well—

"Somebody said, 'A man?' And then—

" 'What man?' "

Eyes round, voice lowered. " 'It were the minister!'

" 'The minister? You mean our parson?'

" 'It were a parson.'

" 'The minister? The minister? Our minister?'

" 'I said, "Good evening, parson," loud and clear, and I said, "God save us all, Parson," loud and clear, and the women ran like deer through the underbrush, and the parson seemed to evaporate, to vanish. He were there, and then he weren't there, and there were only the mist hanging over the pasture.'

"And then the questions came, 'The minister? And he were there with the three witches—Good and Tituba and Osburne? Are you sure?' Then the answer came. 'Oh, it were a proper parson, all in his black clothes and steeple hat.' "

Tituba thought, I see what troubles John. If they're getting ready to say that the master is a witch, then he'll turn on us before he ever lets himself be accused. It was pleasant in the barn. The mare let her breath out with a snuffing, blowing sound, and the cows mooed gently. The chickens scratched in the hay, clucking to themselves, and a broody hen flew up squawking, feathers ruffled.

"Hush yourself," Tituba cautioned the hen. The hen quieted as though it had understood her.

John shook his head in disapproval. "You should stop talking to the animals. That hen acted as though she knew what you said. You could get us hanged if anybody heard you."

"Everybody talks to animals. Mercy Lewis talks to that farmhorse of Master Putnam's—I've heard her."

"Yes, but nobody says she's a witch. The folk are saying that you are the one who bewitched the girls. They say it's a very strange happenstance that the minister's cows never sicken or go dry. His pigs is always well. His garden bursts with vegetables, and the fruit hangs so heavy in his orchard the trees are bowed down with it. His hens lay eggs where you can put your hand to them right away. Nobody has to hunt through the bushes for eggs at the minister's. They've seen you go right to the eggs as though you knew where to find them."

He sighed, "It's these things that will get us hanged—for nothing."

"We will not be hanged."

"What will stop them?"

"I don't know. I'm not a witch. How could I be a witch and not know it? I keep things clean for the animals, and I feed them. That's why everything seems to run smoother here. Hard work is what makes this place run smoother. Those farmers' wives could make their places run smoother if they did more work themselves. They leave everything to the bound girls, and they box the girls' ears if they're angered about something. Then the girl spills the milk because she's cross with her mistress. She forgets to feed the pigs. She gives spoiled food to the chickens. She knows there's a hole in the fence, but she doesn't say so, and when she sees the pigs go through, she looks the other way. And the cattle roam—and—"

And yet she felt uneasy. John helped her fill the woodboxes, and then he went off to Ingersoll's.

Afterwards, before anyone else was up, she filled a small bowl with water, carefully floated some fine oil on its surface, just a thin layer so she'd have a bright surface to look at but no glitter to it. She sat down at the table and looked into the bowl, stared into it, her gaze fixed, unwinking.

She waited, staring. She experienced another vision. She saw herself. She was standing on a table or a bench. People were staring at her. She had seen this scene before in the horse trough. Only this time she could see the master. He was way off to one side, and he was sitting at a table writing, writing, writing, very steadily.

When the master came into the room, she was still sitting at the table. She was no longer staring at the bowl of water; she was looking towards the fire. Her gaze was contemplative.

The master drew back slightly. Then he said, "What are you doing?"

"I was trying to decide whether the oil be rancid, master," she said.

Chapter 16

MEN HAVE wished they might see angels and converse with them. God hath been provoked with them for their curiosity and Presumption, and hath permitted Devils to come unto them, whereby they have been Deceived and Undone—"

Reverend John Hale, of Beverly, was speaking. Tituba caught words and phrases. This had been another day of prayer and fasting. Tall, thin Reverend Deodat Lawson and stout Reverend Nicholas Noyes, of Salem Town, had been praying and fasting all day with the bewitched girls and their families.

Now they had come to the master's house. They were on their knees in the keeping room. Goody Sibley and Mary Walcott were there, Mistress Anne Putnam, and Anne Putnam, Jr., and Mercy Lewis, and Elizabeth Hubbard.

Reverend Hale went on praying, "Let them that have been guilty of Explicit Witchcraft now also repent of their monstrous and horrid evil in it. If any of you have (I hope none of you have) made an Express Contract with Devils, know that your promise is better *broke* than kept; it concerns you that you turn immediately from the Power of Satan unto God—"

Abigail screamed suddenly, a blood-curdling sound. Reverend Hale continued, "Oh, Lord, help us against this unaccountable Enchantment; we beseech Thee not to let this spiritual Plague go further—"

Abigail shouted, "I will not sign the book. I will not sign the book—" and ran around the room, leaping and shouting as though she had taken leave of her senses. Mercy Lewis joined her, and Mercy's shrieks were so high in pitch and so great in volume that they hurt the eardrums. Elizabeth Hubbard cried out that there were rats swarming around the floor, a whole regiment, an army of them, some red and some black. "Look at them," she said, pointing, "look at them."

Tituba looked in the direction in which Elizabeth pointed, half-expecting to see an army of rats.

Reverend Hale stopped praying and stood up. So did everybody else. They could not continue with such a confusion of sounds, such screams, such dashing back and forth and running up and down.

Abigail gave a great shriek, covered her eyes with her hands, and fell to the floor with a thud. She lay there as though she were dead. Mercy Lewis fell down beside her.

The master's face seemed both to lighten and darken. His voice came out suddenly and harshly, "The touch test!" he said. "The touch test!"

He grabbed Tituba by the arm and pushed and pulled her towards Abigail. "Touch her," he shouted, tugging at her arm. "Touch her!"

Tituba bent over and touched her lightly on the forehead, to see if her forehead felt hot; and then she touched her arm—it felt stiff and hard. As Tituba touched her, she felt the stiffening, the hardness go out of Abigail's arm. It became soft and pliable, like human flesh.

She thought, confused, I did that. I touched her and she has recovered. Abigail blinked and sat up. She rose to her feet, and went and sat down on the settle. She adjusted the skirt of her long gown neatly about her feet.

Parris ordered Tituba to touch Elizabeth Hubbard who was sitting on a stool, rocking back and forth, eyes closed, howling like a dog. When Tituba touched her, she too opened her eyes. She adjusted her cap, fingered her neck cloth to see that it was in place, and sat silent.

For the first time since the bewitchment began, Tituba was frightened, so frightened that she felt a trembling inside herself. Perhaps I am a witch, she thought, and I did not know it. Perhaps what they said was true—Good and Osburne and I are witches. Then her spine stiffened. This is nonsense. I am no more a witch than the master is a wizard.

They were all staring at her with hate and with fear—it showed in their faces, in their eyes. The master shouted, "Why do you hurt these children? Why do you do it? Why? Why?"

"I have done nothing," she said. "You know I have done nothing, master."

She was so upset that she had only a blurred memory of their leaving. She was certain that they backed out of the keeping room, that they kept their faces turned towards her as they put on their cloaks and wrapped their shawls tight around their heads or bundled themselves into their greatcoats.

After they left, the master threatened her, saying he would see her hanged unless she confessed to the sin of witchcraft.

She kept saying, "I have done nothing, master. I have done nothing."

He said, "Well, I will now leave you, and then you are undone, body and soul forever." He said this in his harsh, angry-sounding praying voice.

But he did not leave her. He stayed in the keeping room. He said, "You will hang—" "You are a witch—" "You will hang—" "You have bewitched these children—"

Then Abigail came downstairs and had a fit and screamed and held on to her throat, saying, "I can't breathe—I'm being choked—I can't breathe—aahhhh—waahhhh—"

"Stop that!" the master shouted. "Stop that!"

Tituba thought he was talking to Abigail, but he was talking to Tituba. "Unclasp your hands," he shouted. "Do you hear? Unclasp your hands before you choke the child to death—"

Tituba stared at him in amazement and then she looked at Abigail. Abigail was watching her through partially closed eyes.

Tituba opened her hands, let them stay in her lap, palms up. Abigail went on screeching and crying out that she couldn't breathe.

"Touch her!" the master ordered. "Quick! Touch her and put her out of this agony."

Tituba hesitated, not wanting to touch Abigail, thinking, If I do not touch her, she will stop screaming. She hasn't the strength to go on like this. Her face is red; her breathing is uneven; she is getting hoarse.

"Touch her," the master shouted.

She touched Abigail, and it was like a miracle. The shrieking stopped. Her breathing became normal. The high feverish color died in her cheeks. Her hands, which had been tightly clasped together, now lay relaxed in her lap. She smiled shyly at Tituba.

I am doomed, Tituba thought. Even if the master were the kind who would risk his own life and his family's safety to protect his slave, even so he couldn't possibly save me from hanging. Anyone who saw me touch one of these girls in the middle of one of their fits, and saw them suddenly become well because I touched them, would believe me to be a witch.

"Now will you confess?" Parris asked between clenched teeth.

"What do you want me to say, master?"

"What is it that you do to these children?"

"She bewitches us," Abigail said. "She and Goody Good and old Gammer Osburne. They were the first ones to come in the house after Goody Sibley baked the witch cake."

"Witch cake!" the master said, horror in his voice. "What devil's work is this?" He took hold of Abigail's arm. "What are you talking about?"

Abigail told him about the baking of the witch cake, how Goody Sibley and John had fed it to the dog, how the dog had yelped and run out of the house. Right after that, Tituba and Good and Gammer Osburne had entered the keeping room. All of them at the same time. "They were the witches, drawn to the house by the witch cake," she said primly.

"You did this in my house?" he asked scowling. "The black art was used—in my house? Why this is a going to the Devil for help against the Devil—"

Abigail, frightened, said, "We didn't know what else to do. There have been so many things, so many strange things— We didn't mean any harm." She wept piteously and ran out of the room.

"I'll have you hanged," the master shouted, glaring at Tituba, "and Good and Osburne along with you. When this story gets out, it will ruin me in the parish." He seized the birch broom and started beating Tituba about the head and shoulders.

Tituba was appalled. No one had ever beaten her before. His appearance was alarming. His face was contorted with rage. His breathing was quick and uneven. He reminded her of a crazed man she had seen a long time ago running up and down through a street in Bridgetown. The master seemed gripped by the same kind of frenzy as he shouted, "Confess. Confess. Say that you're a witch."

He kept aiming terrible blows at her head, her neck, her ears. This shocked her because she felt he was deliberately trying to injure her. She cowered away from him, thinking that this was more than the hurt to her flesh—the dull ache of her head, the ringing in her ears, the bruised places on her neck. This was an unspeakable hurt to the spirit, to the soul.

She cried out in a hoarse voice, "Yes, master, yes, I am a

witch," and thought, Now I am one with the broken-spir-
ited horse and the beaten dog. In the cane fields I saw a
naked slave whipped until the color of the skin on his
back changed from dark brown to crimson. Now I am
that hard-used slave.

Apparently he did not hear what she said, or else he did
not understand her. He went on beating her and went on
shouting, "Say that you're a witch." When he stopped it
was only in order to catch his breath.

She nodded at him. Then she said clearly and distinctly,
"Master, stop. What is it you want me to say?"

"Say that you're a witch."

"Very well, master. I am a witch."

"Where do you go at night?" he demanded.

She felt as though he had looked into her mind. Did he
really know that every night in her dreams she went back
to Barbados? Every night she saw the island lying in the
sun, the yellow-white coral coast line blazing in the sun.
She saw the blue water, the palm trees. She dived into the
water and could see all the way to the bottom, and she
caught a fish between her hands, and it felt as though she
were holding a long wiggle. Her hands clutched at it,
trying to hold it, and the feel of it always made her laugh.

"How could I go anywhere at night, master?" She said
this in a low voice. "I am here at night."

"Your shape could be elsewhere. The Putnam child
says your shape comes in the night and pinches her, and
pricks her with a thorned branch."

He quickly outlined what it was she was to confess to
having done. She had made a pact with Satan. She had
signed an agreement with him, signing it in her own

blood. Satan had dipped a pen in her blood and she had signed, and then Satan had given her the power to travel through space, to enter houses, to go where she pleased. She could sit here in the keeping room, and people would see her sitting at the spinning wheel, and yet at the same time she could be at Deacon Putnam's, pinching Anne and choking Mercy Lewis. She, Tituba, could be in two places at once.

"And I would not know this, master?" she asked humbly.

"You must know it." He walked up and down the room. "The folks say you spin linen yarn faster than others do. You weave on the loom faster than others do. You can see into the future. You told Mary Warren that she would lose her shawl and she did."

"That girl is like a chicken. She could lose her head and not know it." Her own head was throbbing; her neck ached from the blows he had given her. She thought, I must agree with what he says.

"But you foretold this, Tituba. You foretold this. This is witchcraft."

Tituba thought, That isn't witchcraft. I told the girl's fortune, not a word of it true. You will marry a rich Boston merchant, and you will lose something of value on the way home. Only a way of keeping her quiet and getting her started out of the house. So she went home mooning along the trodden path, thinking I'm going to marry a rich Boston merchant—and what happened, well, she probably ran the horse right under the branches of a tree, and her shawl got pulled off, and she was dreaming about her good fortune and didn't miss the shawl until she got down from the horse and Master Proctor shouted, "Be ye gone daft? Where's ye head covering?" Or perhaps her head felt cold, and then she shivered and shook and Abigail had already told her that Betsey and I could "see" things before they happened so she thought I said she would lose her shawl.

"They say you can cure sickness better than Dr. Griggs. Where would this power and this knowledge come from except from Satan? All things go hand in hand —kill and cure, sleep and wake, life—and—death—"

He started walking up and down again. "And now," he said, "what familiars have you beside the cat?"

"I have none, master. The cat is an ordinary cat." She said this softly, not wanting to anger him.

"You have the cat," he said, just as though she had not spoken. "And what else?"

"I have nothing, master. The cat is not my familiar." Again he paid no attention to what she said.

"When you journey," he said, "how do you go?"

She shook her head. The movement made her wince, and she held on to her neck. "I do not know."

He said, "You ride a broomstick. And what of your sister witches?"

"I have no sisters," she said.

"I mean Good and Osburne. Where do they ride? How do you go? Are all three of you on the same broomstick or pole?"

She did not answer, and he made a threatening motion with the broom. She said hastily, "I don't know how I go—I go—I go to Barbados, to the island, in my dreams. That is all. Only in my dreams."

"Then you admit you can be in two places at once," he said. She made no reply and he said, "If you fly to Barbados every night and yet you are here in this house, then you can be in two places at once. You have just said so. I will have to report what you have told me." He sounded satisfied. "There will have to be a hearing."

He went into his study and closed the door. A few minutes later he went up the stairs. She followed him quietly, and stood out of sight in the hall. The door of the mistress' room was open, and she could hear them talking.

He must have told her that Tituba had confessed to being a witch, for the mistress was saying, "But who will look after me? I will die without Tituba."

"Abigail is old enough to do what Tituba does."

"Abigail? She is only a child, envious and sulky. She will never be able to look after anyone. All of her thoughts are for herself. And poor little Betsey is sickly. The child keeps getting thinner and thinner. Her eyes are so sad. She shivers all the time. And without Tituba—"

Tituba, standing outside the door, thought, "Without Tituba?" Why would they be "without Tituba"?

The master said, "I cannot have her here any longer. The Village talks of nothing else. They say the minister's slave is a witch. His daughter can fly. She's bewitched. Whenever Abigail is at the ordinary, she is taken in a fit, growling and barking like a dog or screaming that she can fly. It is better for all if an end is made of this ungodliness."

"I do not believe that Abigail is bewitched."

"If you had seen her as I have—" He stopped talking and started walking up and down. His footfalls came quite clearly to Tituba's ear. "Sometimes she looks as though she were flying. Sometimes she seems to be a cat, and she mews and hisses and looks for all the world like a cat. This is bewitchment. And right here in the parish house."

"I do not believe it," the mistress repeated. "Abigail is a strange child. She may want more love and attention than we have given her. And perhaps she should have had more to do."

"We've treated her like our own child."

The mistress said sadly, "That is never possible. There is always a difference." And then, "Samuel, stay still. It wearies me to watch you walk up and down and back and forth in so small a space as this room."

He stood still for a moment, and then he started pacing back and forth again. "Just now Tituba confessed to me that she was a witch and that she and Good and Osburne have been afflicting the children."

"How did Tituba come to say this?"

"I charged her with the crime of witchcraft and she admitted to it," he said. "I cannot keep her here any longer. It is dangerous to have her here. The farmers say that this witchcraft started under my roof, and this proves I am not righteous enough to withstand the attacks of Satan. They tell frightening stories of dealings with the invisible world that went on here in this house. Tituba says she is the witch who started all of this."

Then the mistress must have sat up in bed because suddenly her voice came so loud that it startled Tituba, and it must have startled the master, too, because the sound of his footsteps ceased. She shouted, "Samuel, you must have beaten her and abused her to get her to say such things," and she groaned and fell to coughing.

The master's footsteps became hurried. Tituba swiftly went down the steep staircase. He must have run down the stairs because she had barely reached the keeping room when he came into the room, calling, "See to your mistress. See to your mistress," and, not looking at her, shut himself up in his study.

Tituba propped the mistress up in bed and gave her small sips of the brew she had made especially for coughs. When the cough had eased, Tituba tucked the covers in around her, put a fresh log on the fire, and was about to go back downstairs.

The mistress said, "Stay a moment, Tituba." When Tituba went over to the bed, one of the mistress' thin hands came out from under the covers. She grasped Tituba's hand. "I don't believe in this witchcraft. This wouldn't have happened if I had been up and about. What did Samuel do to you to make you say you were a witch? Tell me," she urged, "tell me." The thin hand pressed against Tituba's hand.

Tituba remembered John's description of the hanging of the Witch Glover in Boston, remembered the master shouting, "I will have you hanged," remembered John's warning, "These are a cold, cruel people," and said flatly, "I do not remember, mistress. I do not remember."

When Betsey was told that Tituba had confessed to being a witch, she said, "If Titibee is a witch, then so am I." The master could not get her to stop saying this.

That night after the Parris family had gone to sleep, Tituba told John that when the master had accused her of being a witch she had finally said that yes, she was a witch. John put his head down on the trestle table and wept. She had never before seen him weep. The sight of his great shoulders bowed like that and his head bent over in defeat hurt her like a knife wound in the heart.

She said, "Ah, don't—don't," and touched his arm almost timidly.

He lifted his head at her touch. "Why? Why did you say you were a witch? They will surely hang you"—his voice broke—"and I can not bear it."

"No," she said firmly, even as she said it not believing it but trying to comfort him. "They will not hang me." She wondered how he would have felt if he had touched those girls while they were having fits and his touch had brought them out of their fits, and a great many horrified people had watched as this happened. If, right after this touch test, the master had accused John of being a witch, and kept accusing him, and beating him, wouldn't he, too, have finally admitted to being a witch?

"They will not hang me," she said again.

He banged his fist on the table in a sudden fury. "I hear what they say in the ordinary and you don't. They're out to hang witches. And the master is going to help them. Don't you understand? He has to help them. He has to be the best witch-finder of all, or they'll hang him for a witch or a wizard. They've never liked him here. The folk are already whispering that he's not a proper minister, that he's a wizard or a warlock. Some even say he's made an agreement with the black man."

"With the black man?"

"Yes. They say that's why the master's garden is always filled with vegetables, that's why his cows always give milk—"

She interrupted him, saying, "Who is 'the black man'? Is he a slave?"

"A slave?" he repeated, astonished. "Of course not. They call the Devil the black man. Quite often they call him the tall black man. The folk here say the master has sold his soul to the tall black man."

"But, John—" she said, and for a moment she couldn't speak; terror seized her. "They will hang you."

"Me? I have not foolishly confessed to being a witch."

"No," she said. "But you are a tall black man."

"What of it? I have always been a tall man, and if folk want to call the dark brown color of my skin 'black,' I can not stop them. What difference does it make? Why are you staring at me?"

"John," she said, urgency in her voice, in her manner. "Show me how Mary Warren and Mercy Lewis and Abigail act in the taproom when they have their fits."

"They do the same things here," he protested. "I showed you what they did once before and you said—"

"Show me again."

"Now?"

"Yes." She sat down on the settle near the fire, watching him.

He stood up, took a deep breath, and then suddenly jumped up in the air, fell down, rolled over and over, clutching at himself. He pretended to be screaming, and then he pretended to be shouting though he only whispered, " 'Ah, she bites. She bites. I can't breathe. I can't breathe. I'll not sign, old witch. I'll not sign.' " He crept under the settles and then out again. He pretended to be a dog and barked silently, and then he pretended he was a horse and whinnied and pranced around the room.

Tituba thought his performance better than that of the bewitched girls. He gave one last whinny and came to sit beside her. She said, "When the girls have their fits in Ingersoll's taproom, you must pretend to have fits, too. Just as though you were bewitched."

He turned on her and shook her, saying angrily, "Am I to say that you bewitched me? You want me to help hang you?"

She got up from the settle, moving well beyond his reach. "Quiet yourself and listen," she said. "In all of Salem Village you are the only tall black man. Mr. Preston's Black Peter is a wizened little man, and Mr. Hutchinson's Black Joshua is short and light of skin. Sooner or later these girls will cry out that you are 'the tall black man.' Everyone will believe that you are a devil—and they will hang you."

"I don't believe it."

"Oh, but they will," she said sadly. "Everything is getting twisted and turned around. Nobody is trying to straighten things out. Some of the folk believe that a devil cut off Mercy Lewis' hair. There must be other folk who don't believe this but they will never say so. They are too frightened."

She paused, waiting for him to say something, and when he didn't she continued, "If those girls should take it into their heads to cry out that you are the tall black man you will surely hang. None of the folk will dare say, No, this is not true. This man is John Indian, the best woodcutter in the Village, the best gardener, the best hunter—"

Again she paused and waited for him to reply. There was no sound in the room save the crackling of the fire. He kept staring at the fire, and finally he said, "If I become one of the afflicted and fall down and have fits— What will that do?"

"Then you could not be called a witch or a wizard or a devil. Unless you do this I think they will look at you and think"—here her voice slowed and slowed and slowed like that of a person thinking out loud, trying to remember something, trying to make a connection between two different ideas—"The-tall-black-man, the-tall-black-man, John—Indian—is—a—tall—black—man—and then suddenly they will all be rolling on the floor screaming, 'Ah, ah, John pinches, ah, ah, John bites, ah, ah, John is sticking pins in me, John was the devil who cut off my hair—'"

He shook his head like a man emerging from sleep. He got up and gripped Tituba by the arm. He gave her a gentle shake, "It is you we must talk about."

"Wait," she said, backing away from him, "First you must promise that you will pretend to have fits."

"I can not promise that. I have to weigh it out in my mind before I can decide."

"What do you have to weigh? You have always said that no matter what happens the slave must survive—"

He interrupted her. "I said no matter what happens to the master, the slave must survive. I never said the slave must survive at great risk to his wife."

Chapter 17

TWO DAYS later, Tituba woke up sweating and trembling as though her body knew something that her mind did not know. She heard a wolf cry —a long, drawn-out howl that sent a prickle of fear down her spine. And then silence.

She got up and went outside. Puss, the money cat, went with her. It would be dawn in a few minutes. The sky was still dark, but it was getting lighter. As she stood there she heard the triumphal honking of the wild geese going North. She thought, Spring will soon be here; it's the first of March, and the ice is breaking up in the coves and lakes and brooks. She stared at the sky, peering, and finally she saw the geese flying in a wedge-shaped formation, the leader out in front.

The cat mewed and started walking in and out under her long dark skirt. She thought, I will have to drive him away. They say he is my familiar and they might hurt him.

She went in the barn, and sitting down on the milking stool, she reached inside her dress and took out the thunderstone. In all these years she had never unwrapped it.

An old man who lived way back in the hills of Barbados had given it to her. He had a thick head of very bushy hair, and it was almost impossible to say where the hair of his head stopped and the hair of his beard started. He gave her the thunderstone because she'd cured him of a fever. He said if she ever thought her life was in danger, she was to unwrap the thunderstone and hold it in her hand. If she felt it move in the palm of her hand as though it were alive, it meant she would live, too. It was still wrapped in a piece of dark cloth, just as it was when she had received it.

She unwrapped it slowly, carefully. The cloth was wound around it rather thickly. She was disappointed when she saw it. It was an unevenly shaped, dark green stone, so dark it was almost black. There was a ridge down the center.

For a moment she hesitated. Suppose the stone didn't move? Could she bear to know beforehand that she was going to die?

Then she closed her hand firmly on the stone. It felt cold. She enclosed it in her hand, making a fist. She sat there for so long, waiting, that she almost forgot what she was waiting for. Suddenly the stone seemed to move in her hand like a live thing, and she was so shocked she cried out and dropped it, and then had to get down on her hands and knees, and feel around in the straw on the barn floor before she found it.

Having rewound the dark cloth around it, she went back to the house. The money cat was waiting for her near the back door. She let him in and fed him, and then she looked at him, thinking what a fine animal he was with his thick, sleek coat of fur and his neat, clean ways.

She picked him up and put him outdoors, and when he tried to come back in, she threw water on him. Each time he tried to come near her, she threw water on him, throwing it in his face. It was a long time before she convinced him that she was not his friend. He kept trying to get near her. When he finally turned away and went towards the woods, his fur was soaking wet and flattened so close to his skin that he looked more like a big rat than a cat. She knew he would never be back, but it was better that way.

An hour later, Goody Sibley came to see her. She said, "Tituba, had I known the way the witch cake would turn out, I would have cut off my right hand rather than make it."

"It would have happened anyway," Tituba said. "There was talk and talk and talk of witches."

Goody Sibley said that since she'd made the witch cake, the talk was worse, louder and with less sense to it. Elizabeth Hubbard had been saying that Good was following her around in the form of a great gray timber wolf.

"As long as she was the only one that said it, the folk could say she'd imagined it. But yesterday Goody Vibber saw the wolf, and so did Goody Putnam. It was loping along the trodden path just beyond Ingersoll's and Elizabeth Hubbard was running ahead of it, running and screaming, and the wolf right behind her, its evil-smelling mouth open as though it were laughing. They said they could see the cruel white teeth gleaming, and its terrible tongue rolled out of its mouth, and drool was coming from its mouth." She broke off and her voice sounded choked up. "You're not safe here, Tituba."

"Because of a wolf?"

"Yes. Cow Harry, the neatherd at Ingersoll's, shot at the wolf. He said it disappeared right before his eyes. And where the wolf had been, there was Goody Good, matted hair all crazy over her face and eyes and smelling so ugly that he said, 'Paugh!' and jumped back away from her, holding his nose. He knew he must have hit her in the leg because she limped away. Elizabeth Hubbard says that it was Good that time in the form of a wolf, but she says sometimes it's you, Tituba, and sometimes it's Osburne. They're going to arrest all three of you."

"Arrest us?"

"Yes. They'll be coming for you this morning." She continued, "You see, they keep asking the girls, Who bewitches you? And they give the same answer over and over, Good and Tituba and Osburne."

Tituba looked around the keeping room. She had learned to cook beans with salt pork, to cope with a seemingly endless supply of fish and clams, and of game—rabbit and deer meat, bear steaks. She knew how to take salt stringy beef, and by soaking it and cooking it slowly, adding onions, a snippet of bay, a pinch of dill, and a handful of rice, she could turn it into a dish so savory that the very smell of it in the pot softened the lines in the master's face. She had made the house clean, and kept it warm, and looked after a sick woman, and—

Yes, but those things did not outweigh the fact that she could spin a fine linen thread too fast, and she could weave too fast. And the money cat behaved as though he understood what she said to him, and being a very friendly animal, he probably did.

Goody Sibley said, "Tituba, they're out to hang ye. If

they say ye danced heels over head with the devil, say yes, ye did, but that ye now sit in the dust in sorrow and repentance. Say yes, to everything they ask. Yes, ye can fly. Yes, ye can talk to birds. Yes, ye can talk to rats. Yes, ye can send rats and cats and dogs to pinch the girls—just keep saying yes, I did, yes, I did, and I am now covered with sorrow."

While Goody Sibley was standing there in the keeping room talking to Tituba, there came a great thundering knock at the door. They looked at each other without speaking, for they knew who and what this was.

The knock came again, and Tituba thought, So early in the morning?

A voice from outside shouted, "Open! Open! In the King's name!"

Tituba stayed by the fire. She motioned to Goody Sibley to open the door. Three men entered. One of them Tituba recognized as Joseph Herrick, a tall, handsome man, who was known as the marshal or constable.

He said, "You're under arrest, Tituba, on suspicion of witchcraft. Where is your master?"

She pointed towards the ceiling, indicating that he was upstairs.

"Call him," Marshal Herrick said to one of his men.

They waited in silence. There were footsteps overhead and then on the stairs. The master came into the room. He tried to look surprised, but Tituba was certain he had known about this and helped to plan it.

Joseph Herrick said, "Mr. Parris, I have here a warrant to apprehend Tituba. I will read it to you."

Tituba heard only a word here and there, that she and

Good and Osburne had been complained against by Joseph Hutchinson, Thomas Putnam, Edward Putnam, and Thomas Preston, yeomen of Salem Village "for suspicion of witchcraft by them committed and thereby much injury done to Elizabeth Parris, Abigail Williams, Anne Putnam, and Elizabeth Hubbard, all of Salem Village . . . contrary to ye peace and laws of our Sovereign Lord and Lady, William and Mary of England, etc., King and Queen."

Her heart gave a great lurch inside her because it also said they were to be taken to Nathaniel Ingersoll's to be examined at ten o'clock. She thought, I will see John again.

"Come along, Tituba," the marshal said.

Turning to Goody Sibley, she said slowly, "There is herb tea for the mistress warming near the fire. Someone must remember to look after the animals—feed the chickens, milk the cows, and look after the mare."

Then she fastened her cloak around her, carefully wrapped her shawl about her head and shoulders. She wanted to say good-bye to the mistress and to Abigail and Betsey, yet she did not ask to see them for fear it would upset Betsey.

As she started towards the door, Goody Sibley said, "God speed, Tituba." The master turned his head away, and she pretended she did not see this. She bowed by way of response to Sibley, and then she walked out of the house, following the marshal. One of his men walked behind her and one walked beside her.

The marshal mounted his horse, and his men helped seat her on the pillion behind him and then mounted their own horses. They took the trodden path through the woods, heading towards Ingersoll's. It was cold and very windy. Snow lay unbroken on each side of the path. The trunks of the trees were dark silhouettes against the snow. Occasionally she heard the chattering of a squirrel, caught glimpses of bluejays, and heard their harsh cries of alarm as they warned other birds of the approach of this small cavalcade. They passed through a big grove of very old pine trees, and the pungent smell of pine lingered in the clear cold air.

To her surprise there were other people going in the same direction. They overtook boys and young men who were on foot, farmers jogging along on heavy slow-moving work horses, women and children riding in crude wooden carts that were drawn by worn-out nags. Most of these people recognized Marshal Herrick. Men nodded to him, women bowed. Each time he was greeted, the marshal lifted his hand in salute and then tightened his grip on the reins, so that the horse cavorted almost as though he were dancing.

These people stared at Tituba with such hostility that she finally covered her face with her shawl, so that she would not see the angry looks sent in her direction. She did not uncover her face until they reached their destination. Then she saw that there was a great crowd gathered on Ingersoll's Common, the open space in front of the ordinary where his sheep grazed in summer. A cry went up, "Here they come! Here they come! The constables are bringin' the witches in!"

Marshal Herrick reined in his horse, and the horse pranced, nearly unseating Tituba. His men dismounted and pushed people away, using the butts of their muskets to clear a space around the horses. They helped Tituba to dismount.

There was a roar of sound at the sight of her, "Look! Look! Here are the witches!" And then, "Die, old witch, die!"

The marshal and his men hustled Tituba through the crowd, into Ingersoll's big house, and up the stairs into a small room near the front. They left a guard at the door, his legs spraddled, his musket held butt down. A sword dangled at his side.

Tituba stood in the center of the small room, looking around. One part of her mind kept noting the contents of the room, the big bedstead on one side pushed against the wall, the small windows, the brisk fire in the fireplace, the bench near the fireplace, the table that stood between the windows with a candlestick and an inkstand on it. Another part of her mind kept insistently repeating the hoarse cry she had heard outside, "Here are the witches!" She thought, They brought me here by myself. I am not a witch and I am not old. Thirty-two is not old.

They had also shouted, "Die, old witch, die!" As she stood there she was suddenly afraid. She felt a tremor run through her body. It was so violent that she pressed her hand firmly against her chest to quiet the dreadful trembling. Her hand encountered something hard. It was the thunderstone. She thought, I have to get rid of it. I have to get rid of it. If it is found on me, they will say it is a charm by which I work magic. I must find a place to hide it.

She took a hasty tour of the room. As far as she could tell, you couldn't hide so much as a grain of corn without its being found. Then she thought, But there's the fire, and stones do not burn. The cloth it was wrapped in would burn, but the thunderstone would not be harmed.

Warming her hands in front of the blaze, she pretended to be seized by a sudden fit of coughing, and bending over, she reached inside her dress, took out the neatly wrapped thunderstone, and tossed it far back in the fireplace, and still pretending to cough, still bent over, she watched the cloth ignite. It burned quickly. She knew John cleaned the fireplaces in the ordinary. He took out the ashes and saved them for soap-making. He would find the thunderstone. She hoped he would know what it was.

Shortly afterwards, there was a hustle and bustle outside the door. Then the master entered the room. He had his writing box with him. He said hastily, "I've come to be sure you are prepared in your testimony, Tituba."

He sat down at the table, opened his writing box, and began to write without saying anything to her or asking her any questions. His quill made a faint scratching sound as he moved it over the paper. She wondered what he was writing and why he had come into this small room where she was. She watched him for a while and then removed her cloak and her shawl and sat down by the fire.

When he finished writing, he got up and came toward her. Holding his quill out to her, he said, "Now you must make your mark."

"My mark?" she said, bewildered.

"When people can not read and write they make a mark instead of signing their names. I want you to make a mark on the bottom of these papers. It's just as though you signed your name to them."

"What do the papers say?" she asked, alarmed. John had taught her to read a little, but she could not possibly read all that small writing with which the master had so thickly covered the paper, let alone understand what it meant.

The master picked up the papers and began to read. "It begins like this: Tituba, what evil spirit have you familiarity with? Your answer to that question is: The Devil. The next question is: How does he come to you? Your answer is: In the form of a cat—" He intoned the words.

"This is not true," she said, interrupting him.

"We have witnesses," he said harshly. "Next you say that you have hurt these afflicted children and that yours was the evil hand that began all this dealing with the invisible world."

"I say that?" she asked. She looked at her hands, at the backs, and then turning them over, held them palm upward and stared at them, thinking, They were useful hands, they were skillful hands, and there was wisdom and healing in them. "I will never say that my hands are evil."

At that moment there was a great hullabaloo from outside. The guard and the master ran to one of the windows and looked out. The master made an exclamation of surprise.

"Come here, Tituba," he said, beckoning to her. "Look at this."

Outside on Ingersoll's Common was a great gathering of people. They were making a path, dividing in two groups, so that there was a clear space. Ingersoll's neatherd, Cow Harry, was beating a drum, head thrown back, stomach thrust forward. She could hear it quite clearly through the window. It was this sound that caused the people to turn aside, to make way for the men on horseback who were riding up to Ingersoll's door. Marshal Herrick and two of his men came first, then two men in black clothing.

She had a vision while she stood there peering out through the thick wavy glass. She saw these black-garbed figures, riding, riding, down from Salem Town. She heard the stamp of the horses' feet, the thudding sound they made on a clear, hardpacked place in the trodden path, heard them blowing out their breath, heard the jingle of harness. And she saw that Death rode with them.

"Judge Hathorne and Judge Corwin have arrived," the master said. "We will begin shortly."

Tituba thought thankfully, I will not have to walk past all those people. All I have to do is go down the steep stairs here at Ingersoll's ordinary, stairs as steep as those at the ministry house, and go into the taproom. I simply walk down the stairs and I answer some questions.

Turning away from the window, the master said, "Now we must finish this quickly. Put your mark here." His long thin forefinger seemed to stab at the paper as he indicated where she was to make her mark.

She shook her head. "It says what is not true, master. I have never hurt these children."

He began to speak slowly, choosing his words carefully. "All confessing witches do just what you are doing now. They confess, and then they deny their guilt. I have written down all the things that you said when I questioned you in the keeping room at the ministry house. All my questions and all your answers are now a part of the record. I am the secretary for the hearings and for the court. According to this"—he tapped the papers with his bony forefinger—"you are a witch. By your own confession."

"I am not a witch," she said. She thought it strange that he was not angered by her denial.

"Woman," he said, "there are shrewd things come in against you. We have witnesses and we have your confession and that is all we need. It doesn't matter whether you put your mark on this paper or whether you don't."

He picked up his writing materials and thrust them inside his writing box, thrust the box under his arm and went out of the room without so much as a backward glance.

After he left she heard someone outside the door talking to the guard, saying that the prisoners were to be taken to the meetinghouse. She wondered if this included her.

Shortly afterwards, the guard entered the room and said, "Put your shawl around you."

"My shawl?"

"Yes. And your cloak, too. We're to go to the meetinghouse, and there's a March wind out there." He chuckled. "Time of madness, March is. Ingersoll's big room can't hold all the folk that have come for the witch trial. Come from miles around. Some of 'em even come from Boston."

She went down the steep stairs ahead of the guard. As they approached the door, she heard a kind of roaring sound. Once outside she saw that Goody Good was just ahead of her, and it was taking two strong men to hold her and to drag her along. Just beyond Good, two strong men were helping Gammer Osburne. They were almost carrying her, for she was obviously so sick and so feeble she could not walk.

Tituba found herself breathing faster and faster, as though she had been running. She had never seen so many people in one place, standing so close together and making so much noise. Everybody wanted to see the witches. Everybody hated them.

The cry went up, "Here they come! Here they come!" and, "Here come the witches!"

She saw farmers in heavy boots. They were accompanied by their wives. The wives had small children holding on to their skirts; some of them were cradling infants in their arms. There were bound boys in leather breeches, and finely dressed ladies who must have come down from Boston, and sailors and fishermen from Boston and Salem Town.

There was always a clear space around Goody Good. She tried to thrust her pipe in the faces of the people who came near her. She cursed them fiercely. Her ragged clothing fluttered in the March wind as she tugged and pulled to get free of the men who held her. People held their noses, crossed their fingers. Tituba saw one man cross himself. She had not seen anyone do that since she left Barbados. There was a Frenchman in Bridgetown who used to make the sign of the cross over himself when he was upset or alarmed or excited.

The constables on each side of Tituba guided her along. They were not rough with her; they simply walked close to her to prevent her escape. Their progress was slow because they had to force a path through the noisy crowd.

The hullabaloo kept increasing. She could hear shouts of, "Die, old witch, die," "You burned my child," "You made my cow sicken," "My butter wouldn't come," "My hens wouldn't lay," "The yarn kept breaking in the loom," "My good man was struck dumb," "Die, old witch, die."

A rotten egg landed at her feet, breaking and giving off a rank sulphurous smell. Someone spat at her, and the spittle stuck to the front of her cloak. She glanced around to see who had done this, and a man standing near her covered his eyes with his hands and cried out in terror because she had looked at him. The bound boys began to chant, "She overlooked him. She overlooked him." And a roar went up from the crowd.

She kept hearing the words, "Stinking witch, stinking witch." She thought if these angry excited people should suddenly attack her and Goody Good and Gammer Osburne could the constables save them? Would they even try to save her? The closer they got to the meetinghouse, the more violent and disorderly the crowd became.

Finally it had become a howling mob. She expected to be knocked down and trampled to death in front of the meetinghouse door. She stood still, awaiting the first blow. Instead there was a ripping, tearing sound—and they all looked towards the meetinghouse. The great oak timber, which had stood propped up against the outside of the building ever since it was erected, crashed to the ground. No one was standing near it. The wind was not strong enough to blow it down. Men said afterwards it had been there for at least twenty years.

The sight and sound of this huge timber falling as though pushed by invisible hands silenced the crowd. Even Goody Good stayed quiet. Tituba thought it would be easy to believe that a god had spoken, a forest god, or some strange god of the Indians, or even the master's god of wrath.

Chapter 18

PEOPLE entering the meetinghouse were silent, still awed by the memory of the huge timber that had fallen so mysteriously. The only voice to be heard was that of Marshal Herrick crying out, "Way! Make way there!", as he led the constables and the three prisoners through the crowd.

The marshal indicated that the prisoners were to stand on a table a little to one side of the pulpit. Good scrambled up by herself, Osburne had to be lifted up, and Tituba climbed up unaided, though she steadied herself by holding onto the arm of one of her guards.

Tituba had never before been in the meetinghouse. When they first came to Salem Village the master had decided that Abigail and Betsey must go to meeting every Sabbath day and that Tituba must stay at home with her ailing mistress. She studied the room, noting the heavy ceiling beams, the fact that the interior walls were of unmatched boards which had darkened with age, and that the windows were so small that very little light came into the big room. It was filled with people. Some of them were standing against the walls; some were sitting on long wooden benches; some were sitting in the windows. She wondered whether John was in the meetinghouse. There were so many people, and it was so dark near the back that she could not have picked him out of the crowd.

Cow Harry entered from a side door, just beyond the pulpit. He called out, "Rise. Rise. Rise for the honorable judges. Rise."

There was a shuffling of feet and a pushing back of benches as the people stood. The judges, John Hathorne and Jonathan Corwin, entered. The Reverend Samuel Parris came in just behind them. Hathorne and Corwin sat down at a long table in front of the pulpit. Reverend Parris sat down at a smaller table off to one side. He placed his writing materials in front of him, his quill, his inkstand, and his writing box. Judge Corwin made a gesture which indicated that they were to be seated.

Marshal Herrick read the warrant again. Then he read what he called the officer's return: "According to this warrant I have apprehended the persons within mentioned and have brought them accordingly and have made diligent search for Images and such like but can find none. Salem Village, this 1st March, 1692. Joseph Herrick, Constable."

When the marshal finished reading, he handed the papers to the Reverend Samuel Parris.

Judge Hathorne said, "We will open with prayer, Mr. Parris."

Tituba tried to follow the master's prayer, but she couldn't keep her mind on what he was saying. Goody Osburne leaned against her heavily, and she wondered how long the sick woman could stand without any other support. The sour smell of Goody Good stayed in her nostrils. The master's harsh voice went in and out through her thoughts like a shuttle going in between the warp threads of an intricate pattern on a loom.

He said that many persons in several families of this little village had been vexed and tortured in body and soul by witchcraft and diabolical operations. When Tituba heard the word "witchcraft," she began to listen closely and carefully.

"The Devil hath been raised amongst us," he said, and his voice increased in volume, "and the Devil's rage is vehement and terrible. We are here witnesses to the sin of witchcraft which is the work of the Devil. We all know that the unrepentant witches who refuse to confess their guilt, refuse to admit their sin, must die. We also know that those taken in the sin of witchcraft who confess their sin and repent, and thoroughly amend their ways and their doings, will be pardoned and live. We ask Thy blessing on this hearing. May the Lord be praised. Amen."

A voice from somewhere in the back of the crowded room said distinctly, "Say yes, you're a witch and you'll live. Deny you're a witch and you'll die." Someone made a sound like a horse blowing out his breath. There was laughter and a low-pitched gabbling from the back of the room.

Both judges scowled. Hathorne banged on the table, using a short stout stick. "We will have quiet," he said, "or I will order the marshal to clear the meetinghouse."

The crowd was suddenly silent, not because of Judge Hathorne's threat, but because the afflicted girls were being led in. They were seated on a bench quite near to where the judges were sitting, not far away from the prisoners. Marshal Herrick indicated that the prisoners were to get down from the table. He showed them where they were to sit. Then he indicated that Goody Good was to take her place alone, standing on the minister's chair. The chair had been turned around so that the back formed a bar where she could rest her hands. When she stood up on the chair and the girls saw her, they stiffened and started to shriek. Tituba felt Osburne tremble at the sound. When Judge Hathorne began to question Goody Good, the girls were silent.

Question: "Sarah Good, what evil spirit have you familiarity with?"

Answer: "None."

Question: "Have you made no contract with the Devil?"

Answer: "No."

Question: "Why do you hurt these children?"

Answer: "I do not hurt them. I scorn it."

Goody Good indicated her contempt and hatred for the crowd that watched her, for the judge who questioned her, and for the girls who cowered away from her whenever she glanced in their direction by snarling her answers. Her matted gray hair hung down, partly obscuring her face. She kept shaking her fist at the crowd, and her ragged clothing fluttered about her as she moved.

At one point, Judge Hathorne stopped questioning her to ask the girls if this was one of the persons who had tormented them. By way of reply, they fell to the floor, screaming and crying out that she was choking them and pinching them. Tituba, who had hardly dared glance in their direction, now saw that they were all there: Abigail Williams, Anne Putnam, Mercy Lewis, Mary Warren, Elizabeth Booth, Sarah Churchill, Mary Walcott, Susanna Sheldon, and Elizabeth Hubbard with her knitting. Betsey Parris was not among them.

Judge Hathorne asked Good how the girls came to be tormented when she looked at them. She said, "What do I know? You bring others here, and now you charge me with it."

"Why, who was it then?" he asked.

"I do not know, but it was some you brought into the meetinghouse with you."

"We brought you into the meetinghouse."

She said, "But you brought in two more."

Judge Hathorne leaned forward and said sharply, "Who was it then tormented these children?"

"It was Osburne," she said spitefully.

"That's right—love thy neighbor," said a voice from somewhere behind Tituba. A little murmur ran through the crowd, and Hathorne gave them a warning glance.

Tituba felt Osburne stiffen with rage, and heard her catch her breath as though the outrage she felt had sickened her. Tituba said softly, "Quiet yourself." She touched Osburne's hand gently and then held on to her wrist with a firm grasp. She thought how dark the skin on her hand looked against the dreadful whiteness of Osburne's skin. Osburne's flesh felt slightly cool like that of a very old person or of an invalid. Mistress Parris' hands felt just like this sick woman's hands.

Hathorne asked Good what it was she said when she

went muttering away from Mr. Parris' house. She said that she did not mutter but thanked him for what he gave her child. Then he asked her what she said when she went muttering away from other persons' houses.

Her answer was, "If I must tell, I will tell. It is the Commandments. I may say my Commandments, I hope."

There was a snicker from the left-hand side of the room. Hathorne's face reddened. He turned to Marshal Herrick and said, "Arrest the person who makes the next unseemly disturbance."

He then called William Good to the stand. This was Sarah Good's husband. Tituba looked at him in surprise. She did not know that Goody Good had a husband. His hair was long, too. He kept brushing it away from his eyes. She thought he looked rather like a sheep and decided that it was due to the shape of his face.

Judge Hathorne asked him if there was anything about his wife that had suggested to him she might be a witch. He said, "No." Then he ducked his head forwards, and his voice broke. He said, "I may say with tears that she is an enemy to all good."

The girls were then dreadfully tortured, and amid their screams and their piteous howls, they cried out it was Sarah Good and also Sarah Osburne that hurt them and tormented them. Mary Warren said that the tall black man was whispering in Good's ear at that very moment. Judge Hathorne ordered the constable to remove Good from the meetinghouse. After she left, the girls were quiet.

"Place the prisoner Osburne at the bar," Judge Hathorne said. Osburne was helped up on the minister's chair, her arms placed so that she could support herself against the back of it.

Judge Hathorne began his examination of Goody Osburne by asking her, "What evil spirit have you familiarity with? Why do you hurt these children?" She denied that she hurt them, or that she had any familiarity with an evil spirit. He then said he had been informed that she had said she was more like to be bewitched than to be a witch. What did she mean by that?

"I was frighted one time in my sleep," she said, "and I saw or dreamed that I saw a thing like a tall Indian, all black, which did pinch me in my neck and pulled me by the back part of my head to the door of my house."

Tituba thought, Mary Warren spoke of a tall black man and Goody Osburne is speaking of a thing like a tall Indian—all black. Why didn't John do what I told him to do? Someone will surely say that John Indian is the tall black man. John Indian is a wizard or a warlock, with the power to cast spells—

There was a sudden violent noise, somewhere in the back of the meetinghouse in the part where it was darkest and most crowded with people. The sound was something between a great wailing cry and a shouting that went on and on, "Wahhhhhhhhhhhh!" and again, "Wahhhhhhhhh!"

"What is that noise?" Judge Hathorne demanded angrily. "Constable, arrest whoever it is that is making such a disturbance in this court—"

The sound came again, and there was a scrambling movement as though people were getting out of the way.

They began to stand up and turn around to get a better look. Tituba stood up, too. And she saw John as he came leaping and running, and going over the benches, and knocking people down, shouting as he came. When he got near the area where the afflicted girls sat huddled together, he appeared to stumble, and fell on the floor, and rolled over and over, groaning and shouting, "Ah, ah, ah, ah!"

Tituba sat down, closed her eyes, and hoped that the relief she felt did not show in her face. John was now one of the bewitched. Though the folk talked about tall black men and black things like tall Indians, they could not now accuse John of being a witch or a wizard. He was now one of the afflicted.

The meetinghouse was filled with cries of, "He's bewitched! He's bewitched! Someone's witched John Indian!"

There was such a tumult of talk and shouts, screams from the women, hoots and imitations of animals from the bound boys—they barked like dogs and mooed like cows —laughter mixed in with all the other sounds, that Hathorne recessed the hearing until later in the afternoon.

After the recess, Judge Hathorne said there would be no interruptions, no laughter, or he would clear the court. Anyone guilty of unseemly behavior would be held in contempt of court.

There was absolute stillness in the meetinghouse. "And now," Judge Hathorne said, "Call the prisoner Tituba."

Tituba took her place, standing on the minister's chair, her hands resting on the back of it, facing the great crowd jammed into the meetinghouse. She could feel the beat of her heart increasing in speed, increasing, and increasing until she felt as though she couldn't breathe.

The questions started the same way: "Tituba, what evil spirit have you familiarity with?"

"None," she said.

"Why do you hurt these children?"

"I do not hurt them," she said.

At this point the girls started shrieking. They fell to the floor, staggered to their feet, fell again, rolled over, creating such a disturbance that the proceedings came to a halt. Abigail leapt into the air; her tongue seemed to be pulled way out of her mouth. People were standing up, watching her, too horrified to speak or to protest. Mercy Lewis started jumping up and down, and her cap fell off, and her cropped yellow hair was a shocking sight. Tituba stared in open-mouthed amazement for Mercy's hair was shorter than it had been before. The girls fell to the floor and stayed there, not moving.

Reverend Parris said, "Your excellency, if you would order the prisoner to touch these afflicted children it will put them out of their agony."

Judge Hathorne nodded, and one by one the girls, limp and apparently lifeless, were carried to Tituba. "Touch them," he ordered.

Reluctantly, and knowing beforehand what would happen, Tituba reached out and touched Abigail, the first one to be lifted up to her. It was like magic. Abigail sighed, indicated she could stand by herself, stood up, smiled at Tituba, and walked back to her seat on the wooden bench.

The crowd gasped. The same thing happened when

Tituba touched Anne Putnam, Mary Warren, Mary Walcott, Mercy Lewis, Susanna Sheldon, and Elizabeth Hubbard. Even though she did not believe she was a witch, it upset her to see how quickly her touch restored them to normal.

Judge Hathorne said, "Why do you hurt these children?"

"I do not hurt them," she said stubbornly, and thought, Why does he keep calling them children? Most of them are not children. Mary Walcott, Elizabeth Hubbard, and Mercy Lewis are seventeen. Susanna Sheldon is eighteen. Mary Warren is twenty. They are young women. Some of them are taller than I am. Abigail Williams and Anne Putnam are children for they are only twelve years old. Little Betsey is only nine, but she is not here.

"Your Excellency," the master said suddenly. "In order to save time—I would suggest—Well, may I read the prisoner's confession? I have it here."

Judge Hathorne nodded. The Reverend Samuel Parris began to read from his papers. There was silence in the big room. According to what he read, Tituba had confessed to hurting the children because Good and Osburne forced her to. She had said that Good's familiar was a yellow bird and Osburne's was a yellow dog. She had also said that she and Good and Osburne rode to witch meetings on sticks or poles. Sometimes they had gone to Thomas Putnam's house and pinched Anne Putnam.

When he finished reading, Tituba said, "This is not true. None of this is true." She wanted to shout, but her voice sounded small and weak even to her own ears. She held tightly to the back of the minister's chair, so frightened that for a moment she could not breathe. She had not told the master any of these things. Who in this room would believe her? It was her word against the master's word. He was the minister—and she was a slave. They would believe the minister.

Judge Hathorne said, "You deny this?"

She nodded. "It is none of it true," she repeated. Her voice was so low in pitch and so small in volume that people leaned forwards trying to hear better. Her heart was pounding in her chest as though she had been running. Quiet yourself, she thought, quiet yourself. She loosened her grip on the back of the chair. She began to change the rapid rate of her breathing. She said the word "free" to herself, and breathed in, and then said "free" again, and breathed out. She said this word in her mind slowly, slowly, until she was breathing at her normal rate.

Judge Hathorne said, "Call the witnesses."

The Reverend Samuel Parris rose and said, "I have here the testimony of Abigail Williams. I will now read it with your excellency's permission."

Judge Hathorne nodded.

The master read, "The testimony of Abigail Williams testifieth and saith that several times last February she hath been much afflicted with pains in her head and other parts, and often pinched by the apparition of Sarah Good, Sarah Osburne, and Tituba Indian, all of Salem Village." He held the paper up for all to see. "Here is her mark, 'A. W.'"

"What say you to this, Tituba?" Judge Hathorne asked.

She shook her head to indicate that it was not true.

"Have you ever pinched Abigail?" When she hesitated, he said insistently, "Answer the question."

"Not in the way it sounds there."

"You have pinched her?"

"Only as any person might pinch a child to—" She faltered, and stopped speaking. She had sometimes pinched Abigail, but she couldn't remember why.

"To what?"

"I don't remember. I think it was because she had pinched her little cousin. I wanted her to know how hurtful it could be."

"Then you have pinched her. This is true."

"But—"

"You have pinched her."

"Yes," she said. "But I did not do this often or make her have pains in her head—"

"You have pinched her. So this testimony you agree is true," he said flatly. "Call the next witness."

"Wait," she said. "I never had to do with any witchcraft."

"Tell us who hurts the children," Judge Hathorne said.

"I do not know."

"You say you never had to do with any witchcraft. Maybe you mean you never covenanted with the Devil. Did you never deal with any familiar?"

"No, never."

"What cat is it the children speak of? Answer. Did you have a cat?"

"Yes," she said quietly, and wondered where the cat was and what had become of him.

"Could the cat talk?"

"No. It could not talk."

"We have searched for the cat who is your familiar. Where is the cat now?"

"I do not know." She hoped he was deep in the forest —as safe as a cat can ever be safe. His fur would lose its sleek shininess, and he would have a strange wildness about him. Perhaps he would never again sit near a hearth, watching a fire.

"The cat could talk to you."

"No," she said emphatically. Her voice sounded out loud and clear.

"The cat could do your bidding."

"No, no." She shook her head vigorously and felt a dull ache that began at the top of her head and reached down into her neck. Any sudden movement made her head ache. This was the result of the dreadful blows that the master had given her.

"Did you talk to the cat?"

"Just as any person would talk to an animal—a horse or a cow. There is nothing wrong with talking to an animal."

"The court is not interested in your views of right and wrong," Judge Hathorne said severely. "We have witnesses who say the cat answered you. Call Mercy Lewis."

Before Mercy Lewis could testify, she began to shriek for she was taken in a fit, which made her body stiffen so that she could not move. When she regained the power to move, she jumped up and down, and her cap fell off again, revealing the short, cropped yellow hair. The crowd yelled, "Touch her! Touch her! Put her out of her agony!" The constables carried Mercy Lewis to Tituba, and at Tituba's touch she was instantly healed of her fit.

Mercy stood up on the table, so everyone could see her. She said, "Tituba's cat is a money cat. A very strange-looking cat. It has shining yellow eyes with green in the centers. Very loving the cat is to Tituba. She covers the cat with her long skirts when she sits down. Three different times when Mary Warren and Anne Putnam, Junior, and I were at the ministry house we heard her say to the cat, 'Puss, are you sure you want to go out into that terrible cold and that high drifted snow?' And the cat answered 'Yes, Tituba, I must be off about my business.' "

Abigail Williams said this was true, and so did Anne Putnam and Mary Warren. Mercy Lewis was about to step down from the table when Judge Corwin leaned forward and said, "I have some questions." It was the first time he had spoken since the proceedings started. His voice was high in pitch and sharp in tone.

He said abruptly, "What is a money cat?"

Mercy Lewis looked slightly confused. "Well, it's all colors, black and yellow and white and gray."

"Why is it called a money cat? Does it have something to do with money?"

"It's supposed to bring a person good luck—a good fortune."

"Do you believe this?"

"I—well—it's what the folk say."

"Answer my question. Do you believe that what you call a money cat can bring a person good luck or a good fortune?"

Mercy Lewis hung her head. Finally, she said, "I don't rightly know."

Judge Corwin muttered something about superstitious

beliefs, and then he said, "Did all of you young women go to the minister's house during the winter?"

"Yes."

"How often?"

"Every day, if the weather was good."

"Do all of you live close by the minister's house?"

"No, sir. Some of us had to go a mile. Some of us two miles. Some of us more than that."

"What did you do there?"

Mercy Lewis did not reply. There was a stillness in the meetinghouse. People bent forward, straining to hear the answer. But she did not speak.

Judge Corwin stood up. He was shorter than Judge Hathorne, but in his black clothes he was equally as impressive. He stood looking up at Mercy Lewis. He said sharply, "You said it was terrible cold and there was high drifted snow. Was this true of the three times you mentioned just now?"

"Yes, sir," she said faintly.

"Yet you all went two miles or more to the minister's house? Why did you go so often and what did you do when you got there?" When she didn't answer he said insistently, "What made you go that distance in the dead of winter? What did you do there?"

There were cries of, "For shame! For shame!" Reverend Parris was standing up, looking as though he wanted to protest but not daring to.

Tituba thought, It will be now. The truth will be told now. Mercy will tell about Betsey Parris and her trances, about Pim, the bound boy, and his fortune-telling cards, and about the dolly that had been made in the image of the Mulenhorse child. She will say that the dolly belonged to little Dorcas Good, and she will tell how Abigail threw it in the fire and how Betsey said that the dolly cried out. Then when they heard the Mulenhorse child had fallen into the fire and been burned to death that same afternoon, Abigail fell down in a fit.

It really started right then. Because it was after that, the other girls began to have fits. Mercy Lewis would tell about the witch cake. She would say that the only reason that Tituba and Good and Osburne were said to be witches was because they were the first ones to enter the master's house after the baking of the witch cake. It would all be told now.

Tituba found that she was gripping the back of the minister's chair so tightly that her hands actually hurt.

"Answer the question," Judge Corwin shouted.

"I—can't talk—" Mercy Lewis shrieked, and throwing up her hands, fell off the table as though she had been suddenly struck down dead.

There was such an uproar that Judge Hathorne adjourned the court until the next morning.

Two guards led Tituba to Mercy. Tituba bent down and touched her. Mercy was lying flat on her back on the wide floor boards of the meetinghouse. At Tituba's touch she moaned and then she sat up. Color began to come back into her cheeks. She ran her fingers through her short yellow hair.

Tituba thought, watching her, The real reason the master and the judges and all the folk gathered here believe that I am a witch is because these afflicted girls seem to be instantly healed when I touch them. Or when Good touches them. Or Osburne. This makes all three of us appear to be witches. It leaves us sore afraid.

Chapter 19

GOOD AND Osburne and Tituba spent the night in an unused building that stood near the constable's big barn in Ipswich. They were the only occupants of this makeshift jail. In one corner there was a mound of hay which was to serve them as a bed. Good showed them how to burrow into it and then suggested that they lie close to each other for warmth. Tituba was certain that she would smell like Goody Good for the rest of her life. But it was cold inside and after a while the smell did not bother her.

When she awakened in the morning, she thought that she was in the keeping room at the ministry house and that the fire had gone out. Enough light came through the cracks in the building to show her that she was sleeping in a mound of hay with Good on one side of her and Osburne on the other.

Shortly after they awakened, the constable brought them pieces of johnnycake and wooden mugs filled with cider. After they finished eating, Tituba brushed away the hay from her clothing and from Osburne's clothing.

Good said, "Don't go to brush me off. Not for the likes of those judges."

Then all three of them mounted the horses that had been provided for them and accompanied by three constables, they headed for Salem Village. Cow Harry met them about a half a mile away from the meetinghouse. He walked ahead of them, beating on a drum. They slowed their horses, forming a procession behind him. He led them straight to the door of the meetinghouse.

The crowd that had gathered inside was bigger and more disorderly than it had been the day before. Again the court opened with a prayer by the Reverend Samuel Parris. This time he said that devils were mustering their infernal forces, coming armed to carry on their malicious designs against the souls of many in this poor village. He repeated his previous statement that unrepentant witches who would not confess their guilt would be hanged and that the witches who confessed to the sin of witchcraft and who repented would live. He said this was according to the covenant which they all held sacred. He closed his prayer by saying, "We are deeply humbled and we sit in the dust in contrition. Amen."

The first witnesses called testified against Goody Good. They spoke hurriedly and fearfully, not looking at her while they talked. They said that she carried the smallpox, that she set fire to people's barns and their haystacks with her pipe, that she had caused cows to sicken and die. She had caused children to have strange wasting diseases.

Two farmers, William Allen who was tall and thin and John Hughes who was short and fat, said that Goody Good had come to them in the form of a wolf and had followed them around.

Good shouted, "You lie! You lie!"

The afflicted girls screamed, and some of them had fainting fits, and the crowd roared, "Touch them! Touch them!" When Good touched them, they were restored to their normal state.

Goody Osburne was questioned again. She insisted that she knew nothing of witchcraft. She summoned enough strength to shake her finger at the judges and say, "It is a shameful thing that you should mind these folk who are out of their wits."

This caused a violent outbreak among the bewitched girls. They repeated her gesture, jumping up and down, shaking their fingers at the judges, and shrieking the one word, "Shameful. Shameful. Shameful."

Judge Hathorne ordered the constables to hold Osburne's arms so that she could not make gestures which would upset the children.

Then Tituba was called to the bar for questioning. Judge Hathorne leaned forward, staring at her. His manner was more unfriendly than it had been the day before.

"What magic drink is this you give to the sick?"

"I have no magic drink," she said. "I make a tea from the roots of iris, and I add a little vinegar. That is all."

"Where did you learn about this drink?"

"In Boston."

"Who taught you to make it?"

"Judah White," she said.

"Judah White is known to be a witch. Was this a witch's brew?"

Tituba did not reply. "Was this a witch's brew?" he repeated.

She shook her head. No one could convince her that

Judah White was a witch. She remembered what a pleasure it had been to look at her—the sparkling dark eyes, the long red cloak, the loving way it caressed the long grass and the weeds. "No," she said. "I know nought of Judah White being a witch. My master said she was. But I do not know that she was."

"You know more than your master?"

She shook her head again, and he abruptly changed the line of his questioning.

"Where do you go at night?" he asked.

There had been a confusion of sounds in the meeting-house. It was a noisy crowd. People called out threats, shuffled their feet, moved benches back and forth. This question caused silence.

"I—" She began and stopped. She had told the master that she traveled in her dreams and that sometimes the dreams of the island were so vivid that she thought she had really been there. He must have told these judges what she had said. Had he told them that it was only a dream? A tremor of fear ran through her.

"Yes?" Judge Hathorne leaned forward.

"In my dreams," she said slowly. "Well, sometimes I dream I go to Barbados."

"Where is that?"

"It is an island in the West Indies. The island where I came from."

"How do you go?"

"I do not know," she said. "I would sleep and dream, and presently I was there."

There were outraged cries of "Witch," "Conjurer," "Hang her, hang her." Judge Hathorne banged on the table with the short thick stick that lay there ready to his hand. "Silence! or I will have this room cleared."

He turned his attention back to Tituba. "Were you a witch in the West Indies?" he asked.

"No—never."

"Were you a witch in Boston?"

"No," she said. "I have never been a witch."

"But you knew Judah White, a Jersey maid, who was a witch in Boston. Did you not?"

She hesitated, and there were screeches and outcries from the afflicted girls. "Yes, I knew her. But I did not know she was a witch."

"She is a known witch. You admit that you knew her, so you knew a witch in Boston." He paused for a moment. Then he said, "Where were you last night?"

"In the jail in Ipswich."

"You never left the jail?"

"No."

"Recall William Allen and John Hughes," he ordered.

They stood up and came forward. William Allen spoke for both of them. He did not look at Tituba. He spoke quickly and kept his head down. People strained to hear what he was saying for his voice was low in pitch.

He said, "Last night I was going home along the trodden path when I heard a strange noise not usually heard. And it so continued for many times so that I was affrighted. Coming nearer to the noise, I saw a strange and unusual beast lying on the ground so that going up to it, the said beast vanished away. And in the said place start up two or three women and fled from me not after the manner of other women but swiftly vanished away out of our sight.

Which women we took to be Sarah Good, Sarah Osburne, and Tituba. The time was about an hour within night. And John Hughes saw the same thing."

John Hughes nodded and moved closer to William Allen, almost knocking him down. He said, "I saw the same thing. We set our mark to the minister's paper as to the truth of this."

Judge Hathorne turned to Tituba and said, "What say you to this?"

"It never happened," she said firmly. "I spent the night in Ipswich jail with Goody Good and Goody Osburne."

"Here are two men who say it did happen. They say they saw you on the trodden path in Salem Village last night. Why would they say this if it were not true?"

"I do not know." She wanted to say that she had heard this story before—told differently. There was a minister with the three women. He had been left out of the story. It hadn't occurred last night but some time ago. There was a low-lying mist on the ground which meant it would be impossible to see people plain enough to tell who they were. Before she could straighten out her thoughts, the judge called more witnesses.

These witnesses spoke one right after the other. Some of them testified to the abundance of fruit and vegetables in the minister's garden and his orchard; some said that Tituba talked to the hens and to the mare and to the cows and that they answered her. Others said she talked to the money cat and they had heard him answer her.

There were women who said that Tituba could spin so great a quantity of fine linen yarn as they did never know nor hear of any mortal woman could spin so much or weave so much fine cloth. They said she never went to meeting and was a Sabbath breaker.

Questioned about this by the judge, Tituba said that her mistress was an invalid and someone had to stay with her lest she be taken with one of her fits of coughing. The master had ordered her to stay at home with her. She looked towards the Reverend Parris, thinking he would say, Yes, that is true. But he moved one of his papers forward on the small table in front of him, and pushed another one back away from him, and never so much as glanced in her direction.

The judge said coldly, "Who looks after her now?"

She sensed that they were about to reach some high point in the trial because Judge Hathorne did not wait for her answer. He cleared his throat, adjusted his cloak about his shoulders and leaned over to whisper in Judge Corwin's ear. Then he said, "Call Mary Warren."

Tituba watched horse-faced Mary Warren approach the table where the important witnesses were asked to stand. She pretended to be so weak and so helpless that two constables had to lift her up on the table, and she swayed a little, and hung her head, and coughed faintly.

Judge Hathorne said, "Proceed."

Mary Warren said, "I—well, I went to the ministry house, and Tituba told me she knew what was going to happen before it happened. She said she could see things. And when I asked her how, she said she would show me. She put a sheep's skin that had been dyed black around her shoulders. She had the chimney all stopped up so the smoke came right down in the minister's keeping room and there was so much smoke we couldn't hardly see.

Then she kneeled down and rocked back and forth in front of the fire."

Mary Warren did not kneel down, but she did sway back and forth, showing what Tituba was supposed to have done, saying, "Coom great Kelah, coom, coom to the meal with seed of each gender, coom." There was a stir in the room, as though people were afraid of the sound of these strange words, afraid that Kelah or whatever it was that was being summoned would enter the meetinghouse. Women screamed, and men started moving towards the door.

Judge Hathorne banged on the table with the short thick stick. "Silence. Silence." Then he looked up at Mary Warren. "Before you continue we will go to prayer. Mister Parris, lead us in prayer."

When Reverend Parris finished praying, the room was quiet. "And now continue," Judge Hathorne said to Mary Warren.

"Something horrid seemed to come into the room. I thought it had wings and a hairy face, and it flew around the room and Tituba called it Kelah. She said that Kelah spoke to her and told her that I would lose my shawl on my way home." She was silent.

"Did you?" he asked. "Did you lose your shawl?"

"Yes," she said. "Yes—" And she suddenly started to howl and fell down senseless, just as Mercy Lewis had done.

There was so much noise and confusion in the meetinghouse, so many cries of outrage, and shouts of "Hang the witch, hang her, hang her," that it took all of the constables and Marshal Herrick as well to restore order. At Tituba's touch, Mary Warren, too, was instantly healed of whatever ailment it was that had caused her to fall from the table.

Tituba thought that surely Goody Sibley would come forward and say that Mary Warren was telling a twisted story about the making of the witch cake. Tituba had not worn a sheep's skin around her shoulders and said those magic words. It was Goody Sibley. She looked for her in the meetinghouse. Though she saw many women, she did not see Goody Sibley.

Judge Hathorne said, "And what do you say to this? Are you going to say this did not happen either?"

"It did not happen," she said. "I did not do this."

"Did you foretell that Mary Warren would lose her shawl?"

"I told her she would lose something—but—" The rest of what she was going to say was lost because the afflicted girls began to shriek and have convulsive fits, worse than any they had had so far. When they were carried to Tituba and she touched them, they were instantly restored to normal.

Suddenly, John stood up. Tituba, looking at him, thought how tall he was and how broad his shoulders were. She decided that Judge Hathorne thought he was going to testify against her, just as Goody Good's husband had testified against Good.

Judge Hathorne said, "Come forward where we can all hear you."

John said, his voice breaking, "Tituba is not a witch. What has been said here about her saying magic words is not true—" and he was drowned out by such shouts and cries from the girls and such a roar of anger from the crowd that he could not continue. Judge Hathorne adjourned the court until the next day.

For the next four days, Tituba and Good and Osburne were questioned. When the court convened in the meetinghouse on the fifth day, Judge Corwin told Tituba that he and Judge Hathorne regarded her as a self-confessed witch. They based this on her confession to Mr. Parris before the hearing and on her testimony at the bar.

When she tried to protest, Judge Hathorne refused to let her speak. He said that she had admitted that the following charges were true: She had made a magic brew that healed the sick. She had a cat as a familiar, and the cat could talk. She had known Judah White, a notorious witch in Boston. She could foretell the future. She had pinched Abigail Williams. She was not a gospel woman and never went to meeting. She could spin more fine linen thread faster than a mortal woman could spin. She could weave more fine cloth faster than a mortal woman could weave.

He said she could be in two places at one time. She could be asleep in the ministry house and at the same time be in Barbados. She could be asleep in the jail in Ipswich and at the same time be seen communing with a strange beast on the trodden path in Salem Village. She could heal the afflicted children of their fits by her touch.

"Is this true?" he asked.

"In one way," she said slowly, "some of it is. But that is not the rightful meaning of it—"

She was interrupted by a sound almost like a trumpet call. "Your excellencies, your excellencies—"

They all looked towards the back of the room. A tall

gray-haired man was pushing his way through the crowd, heading towards the table where the judges were sitting.

"What do you want?" Judge Hathorne asked.

"I want to address the court on the subject of Tituba. I am Samuel Conklin, a weaver. I come from Boston."

"Well?" Judge Hathorne said.

Samuel Conklin said that Tituba had been hired out to him in Boston by the Reverend Samuel Parris. He said she had deft quick-moving hands that felt things or touched things, not roughly and abruptly, but with an examining, feeling gesture, as though inquiring into the nature of the object being touched, discovering its needs and how it could best be handled. This held true whether the object was a piece of wood, a child, a fish, or a jar of water. This was not witchcraft. Some people had this kind of ability naturally.

Judge Hathorne said, "Mr. Conklin, what has this got to do with these charges of witchcraft to which Tituba has pleaded guilty?"

Samuel Conklin ignored the question. He said he thought the court should know that if Tituba could spin and weave faster than most women it was because he, Samuel Conklin, had taught her. She had the good strong hands of a weaver and she knew how to use them. He had never known her to practice witchcraft. He doubted that anyone else had either.

He finished by saying tartly, "I have listened to the evidence against her. It has as much value as a bucket of broken shive—which is to say no value at all for shive is the stem of the flax that we throw away."

It took Marshal Herrick and all the constables to restore order. The constables lifted their muskets to keep the crowd back.

Judge Hathorne said, "Mr. Conklin, this court has not asked your opinion on the value of the evidence presented to it. Now get you back to Boston before I hold you in contempt. Marshal Herrick, have a constable escort this weaver to the outer reaches of Salem Village. See that he sets his horse on the trodden path headed for Boston. This court will now recess."

Late that afternoon, the court convened again. Judge Hathorne said that he and Judge Corwin were ready to announce their decision. Good, and Osburne, and Tituba were helped up on the table where the important witnesses had stood.

The three women stood close to each other, swaying slightly because Osburne was unsteady on her feet. Tituba was certain from the way Judge Hathorne's voice lingered slowly over the first words he spoke that the judges had decided that she and Good and Osburne were guilty of witchcraft. Master Parris kept his head turned away, but the afflicted girls stared at her, round-eyed, white-faced, silent.

Judge Hathorne said that the three witches, Good and Osburne, who had not confessed to being witches, and Tituba, the self-confessed witch, stood charged on behalf of their majesties with feloniously committing sundry acts of witchcraft at Salem Village on the bodies of Elizabeth Parris, Elizabeth Hubbard, Abigail Williams, and Anne Putnam of Salem Village . . . contrary to the peace of our Sovereign Lord and Lady, William and Mary of

England. They were to be sent to their majesties' jail in Boston where they would be confined.

There was a great roar from the crowd and shouts of "Hang the witches! Hang the witches! Hang the witches!" "No! Burn 'em! Hanging's too good for 'em! Burn 'em! Burn 'em!"

The constables helped the three women down from the table and hustled them out of the meetinghouse, as the crowd continued to shout.

Again they spent the night in the jail at Ipswich. Tituba tried to sleep and couldn't. She fingered pieces of the hay they were lying on, crushing it between her fingers, thinking that if she could only find something for her hands to do she could comfort herself. Her mind was fretful; it would not stay put: she thought about John, and Mistress Parris, and wondered what had happened to the money cat and if anyone fed the chickens. She kept asking herself the same question, again and again. How could anyone believe she was a witch? A witch?

It was bitterly cold. She drew closer to Goody Good and to Osburne in an effort to get warmer. Finally she dozed.

They left Ipswich early the next morning. There was snow on the ground; the ponds and small coves were frozen. Once again Tituba was aware of the darkness of the forest. She and John and the master and the mistress and Abigail and Betsey had followed this same route when they went from Boston to Salem Village. They had made the trip on horseback, just as the marshal was making it now.

All that day as they traveled towards Boston, she kept trying to sort out what had happened and lay it straight in her mind. She knew she wasn't a witch. She had told fortunes when she knew she shouldn't have. She had not stopped the girls from inducing trances in little Betsey Parris. She should have gone straight to the mistress and told her what they were doing. She had had doubts about the making of a witch cake. She had let Goody Sibley convince her it would be a good thing to do.

Right after the making of the witch cake, she and Good and Osburne entered the house, and the girls had named them as the witches who were torturing them. She told herself that it was a waste of time to try to place the blame for a thing like that.

She thought about the girls and the amazing fits that made everybody crowd around them and pity them and exclaim over them. Would they stop accusing people of bewitching them now that she and Good and Osburne were in jail?

It was dark when they arrived in Boston. The jail-keeper was a fat red-faced man named Peter Wardle. He welcomed them with chuckles, saying, "Ha! Three witches, eh, constable? Do they ride on broomsticks? Will they ride out over Boston Harbor tonight? Ha!"

He escorted them to a small room. It was cold inside and very dirty. The smell was indescribable.

"Never had three witches before," he said cheerfully. "One's sick. Ha!" He pointed to benches against the wall where they could sleep. Then he was gone. He took his lantern with him, leaving them in total darkness.

They had never, any of them, been so miserable before. They were cold. They were hungry. They were dirty. Osburne was too ill to stand up.

They had been there only two days when Tituba heard the terrible clanking sound of chains being dragged across the stone floor of the corridor outside their door.

Wardle unlocked the door and said, "I got to chain you. I got orders from Salem Village. Those witched girls say you're floatin' around 'em at night. A-pinchin' of 'em."

Good said fiercely, "I'd pinch 'em if I could. Jailer, you know we're here in this jail all the time. Every night. Every day."

"I do indeed," he said, chuckling. "I do indeed. But the orders has come, and when the orders has come, I do what the orders say. If the orders say Wardle chain the witches, then Wardle chains the witches."

Tituba noticed that he did not chain Osburne. He pretended to. And though he attached a chain to Good's leg, he did not chain her to the wall. She could move freely though the clanking of the chain would accompany her every movement. Then he stood looking down at Tituba and he frowned.

"I don't have to chain Tituba. She's a reformed witch. She don't fly no more." He said, "Ha!" and pretended he was flying as he went out of the door. He was back in a few minutes with three blankets. "One apiece," he said.

He lingered in the doorway, staring at them. Finally he said, "Be a lot more witches in here before the week is out. They're catchin' witches in Salem Village just like they was chickens on a roost."

Tituba did not believe him. But he was right. As the days and weeks passed, more and more people from Salem Village were brought to the jail in Boston, charged with witchcraft. The jailer laughed whenever he saw Marshal Herrick arriving. "More of the Salem witches, eh?" he'd say. "Well, bring 'em in. We'll soon have to build a bigger jail."

That summer some of the people charged with witchcraft were hanged. Goody Good was one of them. Tituba heard that she had stood in the hangman's cart and looked straight at one of the judges and said calmly and with great dignity, "I am no more a witch than you are a wizard."

During this time of terror and sadness, Tituba made herself keep busy. Samuel Conklin, the weaver, came to see her in the jail in Boston and brought her news of John. At least once a week, the weaver brought her a loaf of good dark bread and a wedge of cheese. He told the jailer that she was a very good cook, and she was put to work cooking for the other prisoners, preparing the thin gruel and the coarse bread that constituted their principal food.

In the fall more of the prisoners were hanged—charged with witchcraft. Then came a revulsion of feeling against the trials and the judges and the kind of evidence that had been used. From that time on, there were no more trials.

But at least fifty people were still held in the prison in Boston. It was bitterly cold. The jailer supplied them with more coarse, heavy blankets—and the cost of these was added to their board bills. But now he removed the chains and the leg irons, even from the prisoners who had been condemned to death. They were free to move around.

Dirty and unkempt, they survived the winter. Tituba, kept busy by the jailer, felt the cold only at night.

In May the royal governor of the colony of Massachusetts issued a proclamation which said all the people in the jails charged with witchcraft were now free. The jailer brought them the news.

They stood in little groups, staring at him and at each other. But with the news of their freedom he warned them, "Can't none of you go till you pay what you owe me for room and board and for the use of me chains. It's quite a bill some of ye has run up. Two shillings sixpence a week. Some of ye've been here for over a year like Tituba here. She come about the first of March in 1692, and now it's May in 1693. More than a year."

"Master Parris will pay my fees," Tituba said proudly.

She was wrong. Master Parris did not pay her fees.

Tituba was the last of the prisoners taken in witchcraft still in the Boston jail. No one had come forth to pay her fees, and she continued to work as a cook in the prison. She was sitting in the dooryard of the jailer's house, cutting up onions to flavor a rabbit stew. As she sat there a shadow passed between her and the sun. Before she looked up she knew who it was. Her master, the Reverend Samuel Parris, stood before her, taller, thinner, almost gaunt.

She stood up and moved away from him, so that his shadow no longer crossed her body. He said, "I came to pay your fees, Tituba, but only on one condition." His voice was as harsh as she had remembered it through the long months she had not seen him.

"Yes, master," she said softly.

They did not argue about the condition. He said he would not pay her fees unless she stood by her confession. This she refused to do. Master Parris left her in the dooryard of the jailer's house.

But that very day Samuel Conklin, the weaver, paid Tituba's fees to the jailer. As Conklin left the jail with her he said, "You have good hands, Tituba. That's why I am buying you. You have the good strong hands of a weaver."

Tituba looked down at the worn, dark hands that had cooked and cleaned and gardened and nursed a sick woman, hands that had been called evil hands. Then she looked up at the tall stoop-shouldered man who had shown such abundant kindness to her. Her mind, tired with trying to straighten out what had happened to her, kept echoing his words—"good strong hands," "good hands."

"I thank you," she said.

The Salem witchcraft trials began in March, 1692, with the arrest of Sarah Good, a tramp, Tituba Indian, a slave, and Sarah Osburne, a sick old woman.

Sarah Osburne died in the Boston jail on May 10, 1692.

During the height of the witchcraft delusion, nineteen persons were hanged (including Sarah Good), and one (Giles Corey) was pressed to death. The evidence used in the trials of these persons was very similar to the evidence described here as being used against Tituba.

On February 21, 1693, Sir William Phipps, royal governor of the Bay Colony, sent a report to his government on the subject of the trials for witchcraft. He said that when he put an end to the court, "there were at least fifty persons in prison in great misery by reason of the extreme cold and their poverty, most of them having only spectre evidence against them . . . I put the judges upon considering of a way to relieve others and prevent them from perishing in prison, upon which some of them were convinced and acknowledged that their former proceedings were too violent and not grounded upon a right foundation."

In May of 1693 all persons charged with witchcraft were pardoned.

Tituba was sold for her jail fees—board, chains, and leg irons—to Samuel Conklin, the weaver. Six months later he purchased Tituba's husband, John Indian, from the Reverend Samuel Parris.

Mr. Parris left Salem Village in 1696 after a long and bitter quarrel with the parish. His wife had died before he left the Village. His daughter, Betsey, regained her health and married when she was seventeen years of age.

Tituba lived on, leading a full and useful life in Boston with her husband, John Indian.